AF245514

WITHDRAWAL

SAUVAGINE

SAUVAGINE

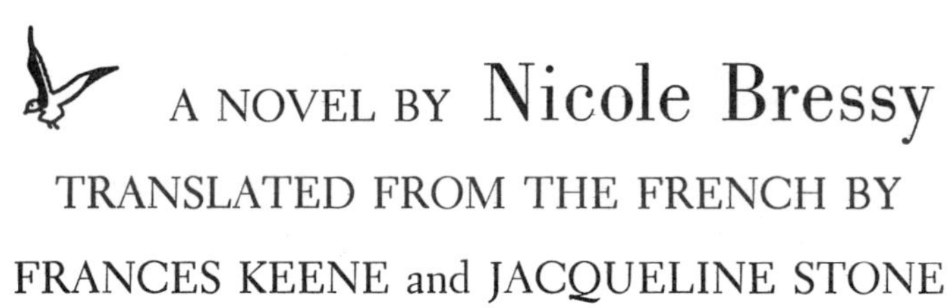

A NOVEL BY Nicole Bressy

TRANSLATED FROM THE FRENCH BY

FRANCES KEENE and JACQUELINE STONE

ABELARD-SCHUMAN

LONDON : NEW YORK : TORONTO

Ogdensburg Public Library
Ogdensburg, New York

Copyright © 1969, Robert Laffont, Paris

Copyright © 1972, Abelard-Schuman Limited (English Translation)

Published in France by Robert Laffont 1969

First published in the U.S.A. by Abelard-Schuman Limited 1972
All rights reserved.

No part of this book may be reproduced in any form without permission in writing
from the publisher, except by a reviewer who wishes to quote brief passages in
connection with a review written for inclusion in a magazine, newspaper, or broadcast.

Library of Congress Catalog Card Number: 78–157982
ISBN: 0 200 71832 0

Library of Congress Cataloging in Publication Data

Bressy, Nicole, 1934–
    Sauvagine.

    I. Title.
PZ4.B844Sau   [PQ2662.R457]   843'.9'14   78–157982
ISBN 0–200–71832–0

And the disconsolate call of the *sauvagine**

Falls sadly on the marsh that the other birds

have deserted . . .

—PATRICE DE LA TOUR DU PIN

*Sauvagine: wild waterfowl that commonly nest in the marshes of Normandy.

I DO NOT LOVE MYSELF.

I feel no pleasure when I look at myself. A few hundred faces like mine make up the anonymous crowd that pours into Paris like a gray river. My body has beauty, but for years now I've been dressing any old way; I've ended up by forgetting it. If a man were to fall in love with me, I'd take him for either an eccentric or an imbecile.

Michel is driving fast. He is as tense as a horse galloping along a sea cliff. Soon we'll reach the Calvados region and he'll slow down, reassured by his native heath. He has just gone through a couple of unexpected days that interrupted his rather monotonous existence. Once he has got over his surprise, he questions me about the future. I guess that he is troubled. Or perhaps puzzled.

When I think of my childhood, nothing polarizes my memories. It's a desert. The only noteworthy event of the entire period was taking my degree. I had done well and graduated with honors, so I was not one of those dunces on whom fate had happened to smile nor one of the truly brilliant to whom our largest regional daily, *Ouest-France*, would have given special mention.

It's hot. My head is throbbing. We reach Lisieux, and Michel lowers the window—he's decided that from here on the air is breathable. He sneaks a glance in my direction.

"Are you cold, Céline?"

His concern irritates me. I'm not used to people bearing down on me with tender solicitude. Yet he has the right and even the duty to worry about me. He's my father. And by chance, at that! My birth certificate and my mother's lack of imagination lead me to believe that he is indeed the author of my being. Poor Michel! To celebrate his twentieth birthday he had the unlucky impulse to deflower a neighboring farmer's daughter. Without knowing what it was all about, my mother lost her virtue at nineteen, thanks to a few rude thrusts of the loins of the young gentleman who suffered, as we say in our part of the country, "the itchings of the virgin soldier." The town notary intervened to reconcile my mother's farm and my father's few ambitions. They were married. I was born. My mother died in childbirth. Michel made the farm pay.

"Papa, I'm hot. Please open your window wide."

"The Normandy air will soon have you back in shape, Céline."

I scarcely know what to say. I have the inarticulateness, at times, of those close to the soil. We don't like to talk much for fear of giving ourselves away, and we only lie readily when we talk about money.

Father, you are a beautiful man. Yesterday I was thirty, which means you are fifty, plus nine months. All my childhood I looked up at the colossus that you are as one looks up to a god, without daring to raise one's eyes too high. But I alone called you Michel: We were cronies despite you. Your youth found me a stumbling block. I never wished to be, you'll grant me that. Your only passion was breeding bulls.

Strangers who inadvertently happen on the marshlands of Carenton do not know that they have breached and entered a closed world that is cut off from the rest of the region by the flat, stagnant, greenish waters of the swamps to the south and, to the north, the cliffsides rhythmically rocked by the sea. Between them there's a long turkey's neck of land stretching toward the Anglo-Norman islands. One far end of the crest shelters Cherbourg, while the other hedges in the fort of St. Vaast-la-Hougue. But the master secret of this land of milk and brine, of this gray horizon hovering like a vast domed shape over the ever-green grass, of these clamp-jawed rustics so ferocious about money that one dare not call them stingy, is that the master of us all is the bull. In the Camargue they raise lean-flanked, blackish beasts. In Normandy we breed monsters. Enormous wild beasts whose sperm is worth gold, who drive a whole farm to despair when one of them has a fever, and whose sale can seal a marriage.

Michel, how many times have you been gored by your bulls? How often have their horns torn your sides, your clothing? You have often owed your survival only to Auguste's taking a hand. Dead drunk with Calvados, he would calm his bull as he did his wife by cursing out the beast in the local jargon and giving it great thwacks on the crupper. Humiliated, you would just pick yourself up off the ground. I would be hopping about on tiptoe nearby, sobbing: "Papa's dead!" and you would merely shrug with impatience.

What was I for you, my father? A creature in a nurse's arms; a small "happening" in sailor blue who breezed in at noon on Saturday only to leave Sunday night. Then, one day "that Lemonnier girl" took the train for Paris. I learned to run away, silently beseeching heaven to have someone follow me, catch me . . . or at least miss me. Nothing happened. After that, inwardly I became a nomad. This evening, too, I am running away, but now I hope for nothing. I no longer have any imagination.

Michel, you are a beautiful man. The years have touched you as they do good brandy—only to improve you. You are the municipal councilor of Valognes, a position you've held for three years now, but do you still have that laugh that fairly bursts out, making the barn rafters ring? It's a long time since I've heard you laugh.

"We'll drive through Caen. You won't recognize a thing. You can't imagine how the city's changed!"

At Caen I feel cold. It is a city full of drafts. Why did you come to fetch me? I look at you without quite believing my eyes. Without you, I'd have died simply because of the wish to live no longer, like a creature who has reached the end of his tether and for whom death is just one more surrender.

Did you sense perhaps that strange call of animals who seek their dying forebears to bring them back by the scruff of the neck, if need be, to a quiet corner where they may die among their own kind? I believe it must be this, for you're a creature of instinct.

We reach the marshes. We are at home. Evening draws in, and the sun is lost amid the glaucous tangle of rush canes, floating grasses, and dead trees. On the instant, the fog rolls in, catches on the branches, high and low, is torn to shreds, and disappears. It skims the water without ever touching it. Legends spring out of the fog. Our local stories are born from this unreal source and are, often as not, swallowed up in it.

"They're going to drain the marshes to reclaim the good earth for pasture land."

"Then what will separate us from the rest of Normandy?"

"So you're a separatist, Céline? You remind me of my mother, your Grand-mère Phellie. She was a *chonane*, a royalist under Poincaré! She ruined us with her baseless dreams."

"Madness always skips a generation. Now it's my turn."

"Oh, she wasn't mad. She was a masterful woman—hard, violent, keeping to herself. But she needed a king. You're a lot like her—physically."

Yes; I hear my father's qualifying adjective clearly! Morally, I'm not "a lot like" anything.

"When you were little, you were afraid of the marsh witches."

"I had the fears others had forged for me. You didn't do anything to free me of them, Papa."

Michel takes on his thrust-jawed look.

We reach Valognes, my little city asleep in its past. The Allied bombs wreaked havoc here. A few private homes are still standing in this "Norman Versailles," hiding their secret lives behind blind walls. Barbey, our local poet, is not dead: He haunts his city, and there's not a soul from Valognes who has not passed his shade after nightfall in the Rue de Poterie or the Rue des Capucins. One evening, as a child, I met him on the

Place du Calvaire. I took off like a frightened deer. A gentle, sempiternal rain bathes our history and regulates our lives. The Revolution of 1789 erected its scaffold on the Place des Capucins, but the rain soon rusted the guillotine and they finally removed this useless object that cast a pall over the passers-by. It's ever thus. We do what the rain will let us do. One mile farther on and we are at Hérouville.

"Can it be five years since you've been here, Céline? Yes. My sister Amélie had just died."

And I, I had just been married.

Hérouville, my house. A long building of dark granite with narrow, small-paned windows dug into it. A blue slate roof rides low over its brow. Hérouville: You are like a surly fellow who has pulled his battered gray felt over his eyes, better to spy on other people. Your north façade is planted with heavy, almost treelike hydrangeas that bloom as they see fit in many rain-washed pastel shades. To the south you boast a rampart of camellia shrubs grown from the few shoots my mother had planted there as a young bride.

But the heavenly side of Hérouville is all that encloses it, warms it, hides it from others: the farm, the outbuildings, the stables, the storerooms, the haymow where I used to frighten the broody hens as I picked up their warm eggs in the crackling straw, that sweet-scented long grass they mow in June when the earth is warm. At least this *was* the heavenly side. For Michel has modernized it. I see long, clean barracks-like buildings that would be hard put to smell of the liquid manure that flows through them. The cowhands—now called "agricultural workers,"—live in Valognes. The old system of renting labor no longer exists. Gone are the days of the annual fair—and not so long gone, at that—when a farmer contracted for his help by the year on the strength found in a man's face, took him on like a slave. Michel, how do you manage to control your rages now when you used to be free to land a worker a flying kick in the backside? There is no one living on the place except Auguste to enjoy this sign of special favor, and he likes it that way. Also, I wonder why the west wind hasn't snatched off the television antenna that insults the roof.

"A fellow from Paris paid me a fortune for the old beams of the fieldhands' mess. There's still the dovecote. I'm going to tear it down."

I cried out loud. "No! Oh, papa, let's keep it. It's like a hunting lodge. I'll turn it into a study."

"You're mad, Céline. There's two hundred years of bird lime and lice in there."

"There are also stones two hundred years old and beams blackened by time. Let's keep it as a witness to the past. I don't want to live on a model farm, Papa. *Please* keep it!"

For the first time in the past four years I find myself wanting something. An imperious wish. I've become used to whims only, vague desires that would vanish if I stretched out a hand, that I no longer know how to want. I am immediately abashed.

Michel looks at me, perplexed. I've finished my studies. He has my diploma. I've written a novel and dedicated it to him. Did he so much as look it over? But then . . . Hérouville belonged to that young wife who died in childbirth, so Hérouville belongs to me. Now that I've learned how to hate, I'll be able to say so.

"We'll spare the dovecote if you wish. I'll have it disinfected. I'll ask the contractor who sent that Paris fellow to restore it. And Auguste will reslate it for you. We'll plant lots of blue hydrangeas . . ."

So I'll have blue hydrangeas. How simple it all is. Father is conciliatory: He doesn't want to cross me. What did the doctor tell him? That his daughter was an alcoholic? I can't quite manage to believe that I should take such a qualifier seriously. Yet it seems a woman's liver can stand only one half-liter of wine a day. And there I was, on the bad days, drinking a half-liter of gin martinis. The doctor raised his eyes to heaven. Am I the only wreck of thirty he's ever seen? No, there are other women my age whose lack of regard for themselves has taken on the proprotions of a cult, still others who have simply dropped their arms and stopped fighting. But then, alcohol makes me sweet and agreeable . . . And what about Philippe? What did he and Michel say to each other? Philippe does not like to feel guilty. He has lived the life of men of his kind, that's all; it was not his fault that I did not know how to adapt. I am the guilty one. Still, I stood by and counted your strokes of luck, Philippe, and I passed from painful stupor to resigned stupor, and it took me quite a while. I'll grant you my moodiness, but after having waited for the end of your first idyll, thinking that it was only a regrettable incident, I had to live through the spring tide of all those that came after. Each time you put me down, Philippe, each time you rejected me, I would collapse and slide a little further. Weakness is comfortable.

However, I've a royalist's, a guerilla-fighter's blood in me. Where I come from, a woman who is rejected by her husband either hangs herself from a beam or accepts her life. But I snapped to—I called for help. Michel came. Tonight, seated beside him, I look at Hérouville-la-Neuve. I need to forget.

14

I get out of the car. Dogs smell my new scent and bark. My house. How could I live for five years without setting eyes on you? I must have been first devoured then laid low by another love than the passion I have for you!

A stocky, black shape moves toward me, stops, lowers its head, raises it. Auguste!

"Ma'am Chéli!"

"Auguste! I'm Céline, the one who used to run after your *'pee-pees.'* Where are all your chicks?"

"Ah, they shit all over. Boss told me to kill 'em."

They have tidied up my father for me.

"Tonight I'm tired, Auguste. But tomorrow I'll come by to take a long look at the animals."

"You're no sweet-scented geranium, I'll say that," he mumbles kindly, looking me over.

No, nor a sweet-scented heart, either. Michel has unloaded my bags. We enter the house, which is fairly ringing with the clatter of plates. Julie has prepared the inevitable *soupe normande*, a soup made with salt pork and cabbage. Its odor mingles with that of the freshly waxed floors. All of a sudden, there they all are: the plate rack, the copper pots, the dark furnishings, the high ceilings. At one time, the great hall had room for two tables, one for the family, the masters, and one for the farm hands. And two menus, too. I can still hear my Aunt Amélie as she bought salted herring: "Give me the very smallest. It's for the servants."

But now Michel has partitioned off the largest rooms. Each one eats with his own, or by himself, as he chooses, except for haying time. But we dine in the grange, for the new room is too small.

We dine between the television set and the window that opens on the camellias. I'm trying to get the feel of the house. It does not have the aura of a woman's presence. So Michel lives alone. All the better. I'll have him to myself.

The soup we are eating is piping hot and overcooked. Michel tucks into the serving in his soup plate. We drink cider from those local half-steins, fat cups of brownish earthenware that weigh heavily in the hand. The cider is fresh and tickles my nose.

"Before I turn in, I'd like to make a tour of Hérouville."

"We'll take a short walk; you'll sleep all the better for it."

I have proprietary instincts. I want to lay hands on my rediscovered domain. We go out. Night is drawing on. It's the time when old people go indoors saying to each other, "The dew is falling." The animals who are pastured close by fall asleep, and their gentle breathing is all about us.

A car beyond the barrier drives by, slows, a head leans out and hastily withdraws, as stupid as a chicken's head and with the same forward-back movement.

"It's Letellier, he's heard the news."

"Strange way to ask after my health."

"Ah, but you remember we're feuding."

Michel has just stated axiomatically: "Letellier and Lemonnier are enemies." We inherit our hatreds along with our patrimony in these parts, and without question. There's not a single old family of our stripe that is not the enemy of at least one other such family and that, for good measure, is not on speaking terms with some branch of its own family tree. When an inheritance is read out, this is the only part a Norman will not dispute.

Letellier knows there's "a misfortune" at the Hérouville farm. The Lemonnier girl who had "done her studies" and married a Parisian has come home. She is ill, and a contractor from Valognes was called in to put a heater in her bedroom. And yet it's nearly the end of April.

Letellier sniffs and prowls like a jackal. Tough luck, neighbor. Your atavistic hatred is as pointless as the erection of an impotent man. My hate is lucid, and I welcomed the force of its muddy waters with joy. It has swallowed me up, but it has also saved me. It is my refuge. I hate Philippe. I hate all those he loves. It isn't possible that my hatred and that of this primate Letellier can be the same! My eyes follow the light of his headlamps for a long time as they fade, then reappear, lighting up the hedgerows. I'm cold.

Philippe, don't come here to torment me. Michel will give you the same treatment he metes out to Auguste when he doesn't mix the bull's mash as it should be prepared.

Letellier's headlamps no longer light up the night. All is at peace.

"Let's go to sleep, Céline. You've lived a long day."

The Normans get up at five and go to bed with the chickens. Time does not weigh on them except with the approach of winter when the white sun is lost in the marshes by five in the afternoon and the animals huddle into the hedgerows to diminish the wind. I can still see them in the distance where they form great white blots in the newborn night. Are they uneasy there in the dark, those heavy milkers? The farmhands bring them in only to calve or when the winters are bitter cold. I still remember what happened in 1953. The hay ran short, and for a long while the sea threw up frozen fish on the strand at low tide. . . .

Michel and I stand face to face, such strangers that we still don't know how to bid each other good night.

I get up on tiptoe, raise my face to his, and kiss him twice.

"Good night, Papa . . . and thanks for coming to get me."

"It was my duty, Céline. You are my daughter."

"I thought perhaps you wouldn't have remembered."

"You must understand—when your mother died I was twenty and I didn't know how to care for a baby. Your Aunt Amélie loved you."

"No, she didn't love me. She loathed my mother, so why should she love me? She sent me off to boarding school when I was seven. I remember her as a hardhearted farm woman."

"Come on, Céline. She's dead!"

"Much good may it do her."

"You left for Paris, and then you got married without letting us know," he said.

"I decided it was useless to announce an event that you couldn't possibly care about. What a pity one can't ask a baby's opinion before creating it! I'd have begged you to take the usual precautions . . ."

I am relighting a fire that has been poorly smothered, and I look my father straight in the eye. How many times I've dreamed of this moment! I enjoy it to the full. Fifteen years late, but now I am the child-judge finally voicing my complaint.

Michel is stunned. I stared at him up and down, my back to my bedroom door, and I know I am in no way like my dimwitted mother nor like the frightened kid he remembers, the one who ran away. But I love him too much. I give in.

18

"You still have a few years left to love me!"

Thus, with a grin, I leap over the moat of my lonely green years.

"See you tomorrow, little girl."

He has just voiced the first endearment of our life.

I open the room I had as a little girl without emotion. My childhood was indeed a desert. I was a child who was convinced that nothing would be given me, and so I wished for nothing. I was as ill loved as those little waifs who, when June arrives, go from farm to farm selling their baskets of wild mushrooms. Full of bravado and my heart at bay, I left for Paris to prepare for my B.A. I arrived at the St. Lazare station in a gray duffle coat. . . . I did not know how to take the Métro. I asked a taxi driver to take me to the Cité Universitaire. He cursed me out because I did not give him a tip. I had had no previous brush with such legal begging. The deputy from the Channel area had "contacts," and I obtained a room at the Provinces of France dormitory.

You repaid him badly, Michel. You seduced his wife. He told me so himself.

The girl who roomed next door was ugly. I had no complexes. She was obliging, and I felt less alone. She was a Communist. I became one.

It was a revelation. Pure product of the Sisters of the Blessed Saviour, I entered the world of atheism with the enthusiasm of a novice. I swallowed it all whole: hatred of capitalism, class struggle; I sold the Sunday *Worker*, I protested against everything. The day I was admitted to the Party, they asked me: "What does your father do?" I hesitated, then stammered

"Farm worker." They were very pleased; if even gave me a certain prestige. My new friends also gave me a taste for fellowship and sharing; they swept me along—I was still too frightened to dare think for myself. A few of them courted me. I said no once or twice. It's well known that a good Communist has little imagination, else he or she runs the risk of being accused of deviationism: They interpreted my refusals as proof of a purely idealistic nature! The long and the short of it was, I was still a virgin. This virginity of mine plagued me like a physical deformity. I dragged it along without daring to face up to finding a partner who would rapidly rid me of so slight a defect.

Poor Philippe, it was you who had the chore of altering the situation. I still remember how surprised you were!

My political peers soon worried about me. The taste for chicanery became, in my case, an acute exegetical sense. I interpreted the texts, I reasoned why. . . . They didn't like this. I don't deny any part of these early experiences. No one tricked me into anything. I opened my beak of my own accord, but I wanted to see what was being put in it, and not being bound by love of anyone, I was sovereignly independent. Any form of authoritarianism wounded me. I quit the Party. That's when I decided to spend a Sunday at Valognes. I stopped to thumb a ride on the bridge at Saint-Cloud. That's where you picked me up, Philippe.

You were going to Deauville. You were so obliging as to make a detour via Caen and there you bought me a first-class ticket to Valognes. You are naturally and effortlessly charming, and it's impossible not to smile at you. I promised I would call on you to repay the money the following Tuesday. And you married me.

Later on, I asked you, "Why did you give me a lift on the Saint-Cloud bridge?" You answered, dazzled: "You were for real!"

I open the bed to icy sheets. My bed is bloated like a notary's belly. It is covered with a big feather quilt. I'm cold. I scrunch down and keep my thighs pressed tight together. My recollections begin to float, to detach themselves from me. Yes, I need to forget.

The silence of Hérouville calms my spirit. How did a lonely little girl wander through thirty years of life without getting lost? My gesture toward my father was the ultimate simplistic act of defiance of my badly managed childhood. Either papa comes, or there'll be nothing. . . . Tomorrow I'll go over Hérouville from top to bottom, I'll move some pieces of furniture, I'll go to Cherbourg to place some flowers on my mother's grave, and I'll start to get Michel to love me.

I'll spend the whole summer here. For the first time in my life I'll have a real vacation. My future stretches as far as the eve of All Saints' Day. I don't want to know what will happen after that. I am incapable right now of caring whether my life goes in one direction or another. From now till then I'd like to relive a *happy* childhood.

I don't like to wake up. I stretch out my arms under the sheets and feel about. I'm alone. Once more, Philippe has not slept at home. No, that's not it. I am at Hérouville. I won't spend my nights alone, smoking, waiting for the sound of a key in the lock to set me free. I would recognize that sound among a hundred others. How many times, Philippe, you would come to say good night to me at four in the morning, bringing me the lingering perfume of the woman you had just been with!

Now I must cope with the sequel to my long period of patience. I cough. Every morning, for a quarter of an hour, my raw throat rebels at what I have been drinking and smoking for the last five years. It's started. Five minutes later I'm crying. Another five minutes and I can't breathe. I know the ritual.

"Céline, what's the matter?"

Michel bursts into my room. I see him through my tears. He draws back in spontaneous disgust.

In this region as in the greater part of our rural areas, everyone in the village is full of sympathy for anyone who has caught clap. But if anyone "has trouble with his chest," it's different. The farm to which such a "leper" belongs is a marked spot, and people will say for years, "There's no health in *that* family."

Julie will have heard me from the kitchen, and from our noonday meal on she will wash my dishes with ammonia, separate from the rest.

I manage to gasp out: "My throat."

"You have a sore throat?"

I nod my head. Michel's tense features relax. I still need another five minutes. I try to smile. He goes off for a pot of honey. By now I've calmed down. I'll remember my father's reaction of disgust for a long time. I try to clear myself.

"Don't worry, Papa, nothing's wrong with my lungs. My doctor would have told you."

Then a flash of genius . . .

"Just listen to Auguste when he gets up in the morning. I heard him a while ago. Well, I drank less than he does, but I have a little bird's throat. That's all."

He smiles, reassured. He prefers having his girl compare

herself to an old boozer rather than suspecting that she might be tubercular. As for me, I've had a lot of practice in humiliation.

He offers me a spoonful of honey. I take it from him almost with fervor.

"Leave me the honey pot; it will do me good. But do sit down. You're so big, just looking at you wearies me."

He sits down, and the bed groans.

"Have you had breakfast?"

"I'm a peasant. I have my breakfast of black coffee and a piece of buttered bread at five o'clock. Then at nine, I have a *collation* of soup and an omelet and bacon."

"I want to have your *collation* with you."

"Don't move. Julie'll bring us up a tray."

My fit of coughing still bothers him. Soon Julie arrives, her suspicious expression in top form. My father places a small table by my bedside. This is the moment to state a new need.

"I would like to go to Cherbourg to take some flowers to my mother's grave."

He is surprised. How is one to tell him that I need to reconstitute a family and that a shared death is an essential ingredient?

"Then you could pay your grandmother a visit. She lives in retirement at Vauville. I tried to rent her enclosures on the bay at Ecalgrain to raise mutton."

"She won't hear of it?"

"There's a coolness . . ."

"Well, obviously. You 'violated' her daughter. Tell me, Papa, are there *any* people who love each other in this part of the country?"

He bursts out laughing.

"You've inherited my way of saying things, Céline!"

"I'll go to see this grandmother of mine, and I'll tell her you are an impulsive but also a charming man to whom she must rent her salt pastures."

"When she dies, her property will come to you."

This is an old habit in our region: People never speak of a piece of land without indicating the future inheritor. Something rarely "belongs to" someone—it is nearly always "for" someone.

"Don't ask me to kill her off!"

He looks at me, laughing. His eyes still betray a certain distrust, but then, too, there are flashes of happy surprise. I'll win him yet. He must love like a tornado, like a free man. Everything is true in him.

"You're a fine match, Céline. Hérouville belongs to you, too."

"You're the master of Hérouville, Papa; what would become of it without you?"

This, too, had to be said, but we'll come back to it. Julie's return dispels our strain. She brings us frothy golden omelets stuffed with pieces of bacon. She looks cantankerous. I think of the old servant Flaubert called "a half-century of servitude." For the first time of her long service, Julie carries a luncheon tray. In Normandy, farmers and even country nobility eat their lunch at the kitchen table. A bed is made to sleep in, die in, and a shared bed is for making children. The only people who get fed in bed are sick people. My father must have thought me farther gone than I am. I enjoy my privilege since it allows me a few moments of intimacy with Michel. I'll try to make them count. Michel devours his food. There, he's standing up already.

"Rest a little longer. I'm going to mend the electric fence in the cow pasture. Cowhands have changed these past years . . . used to be old drunkards, tellers of tall tales; now it's an electric fence!"

"Go ahead: electrocute your livestock, you killer of little chicks, you. You snatcher of deputies' wives!"

"What? What's that?"

I'm openly pulling his leg with my histrionics. I wink at my public and beg it to find me amusing.

"Yes, sir, the lady's husband told me so himself, he did. He even found the joke rather bitter."

"That one. Some day I'll break his back for him."

"And spend the rest of your youth and vigor in perpetuity in the underground solitary of some local jail! Judges adore wronged husbands, it seems, since they believe they all belong to the same fraternity. Instead, Michel Lemonnier, why don't you change mistresses?"

"I've already thought of it."

"But why do you two carry on out-of-doors? It seems you could be seen from the living-room windows. After all, you're not responsible for the sex education of the virgin sons of the soil hereabouts!"

"That's the way she wants it. I've never known a woman to hate her husband as fiercely as that one. He's a real mule, he is. He manages to get it up once a year, after the annual cattle show when he's so drunk he forgets he's impotent."

"Haven't you ever caught cold?"

Michel explodes with laughter, I start laughing, too; we're

like a couple of silly adolescents whispering mild obscenities behind the monitor's back. He looks at me as if he were looking at Prince after he'd won a blue ribbon. I think he's going to love me.

"But, Céline, making love out-of-doors is healthful! You people in Paris, all you have is those dreary hotels where you have to close the shutters *and* the windows. Me, I'd stifle!"

"And if you felt like it between noon and two o'clock, you'd have to wait for an empty bed by taking a walk up and down the sidewalk in front. Papa, promise me you'll never leave your native Normandy!"

We are laughing helplessly once more. Michel is happy to have found this unexpected comrade. Hérouville must often have seemed empty to him. I throw my arms around him which surprises him completely. Time spared him my childhood adoration, and I am reassured. I don't feel completely useless.

"On your way to those electric fences, Papa. I'm going to get up."

"See you . . ."

My bed is warm. I could slide all the way down and slack about till afternoon.

How many mornings haven't I wasted that way! Philippe, you gifted me with solitude. I killed time by telling myself over and over that all effort was useless since you no longer loved me. I was happy enough in my solitary bed. Our social engagements were my cross. You are well-known: We had to accept and return invitations. Women are fierce. I had become their spectacle. They tore me to shreds. How many of those who laughed at my distress have known a similar fate since then?

Only now have I begun to understand you, Philippe. You are

the man eternally in love with love. Each woman suggests another facet of the experience to you, and you cannot resist. You are an exquisite man, just as a sea anemone seen from a distance is exquisite! I hate you, but I, too, have faults. You are a creature before whom one must show proof of courage. Or of egoism. One must flee you: No woman can bloom in your presence. I got hung up on you—I wanted you to be both for and against yourself. This is what it's brought me.

I get up. The farmyard is quiet; everyone is working in the fields. There is no large bathroom, only the basin and a w.c. When I turn on the water, it's icy. I give myself a sponge bath, and the chill makes my face tense. I put on a body stocking, slacks, and a pullover. I'll get some clothing at Cherbourg. I go downstairs. Julie does not utter a word. She knows Michel's habits; I must be on my guard.

"What are we having for lunch, Julie?"

"How should I know?"

What little blood I have flares in my cheeks.

"Julie, I'm the mistress here, whether you like it or not."

My heartbeat has quickened with anger. Or is it weariness? Is it laziness? I'd so like to let my hands go limp and at last be the person to whom everything is given: smiles, tenderness, joy. Instead, I'm the one who seizes everything the hard way, the one who grapples and who obtains damned little for her pains. Never quite enough to constitute a victory. How can people expect me to live by trying to make others love me?

Auguste! He is already soused. I go toward him. Our most handsome bull is about to leave for the cooperative that handles artificial insemination. He is being curried. Such a to-do for such a meager mating! Drunk as he is, the old cowhand talks to his great beast, brushes him till his coat gleams. The monster bats an eye and ponderously shifts his ton and a half of weight. He smells me and utters a bellow. Auguste pats his flank. The creature starts turning on himself and paws the ground. He is reverting to the wild state. Auguste raises his voice, curses him out in dialect, and Prince calms down like a pet dog.

I never get enough of watching the high drama of this fragile old drunk flirting with death.

"Where's the master, Auguste?"

He does not hear me.

As soon as his hands touch Prince, they stop trembling. His bloated face, with its dirt-caked wrinkles like a swallow's nest, takes on an expression of beatitude. The universal expression of the family of alcoholics.

I leave them, almost on tiptoe. I need to take a look at Hérouville from a distance in order to get the most out of it.

Red hawthorne lights bouquets of fire against the tender green of the hedges, the pastures are all carpeted with flowering gentian, the low-branching apple trees are plumped out with bloom, making pink and white balls that roll away down the vales and snuggle up here and there against the little hills that mark the horizon with their pastel blue.

I lean against a rail fence, hoist myself up. I'm tired, and now my hands are trembling. I have scarcely the courage to open my eyes wide to see my house, ringed by its pale hydrangeas. This is the season for first communions. Soon the white veils will fly into each farm's courtyard; a calf will be slaughtered, and the kitchens will smell deliciously of sugar. I am a stranger here. These people will no longer accept me as one of their own. They will respect my acres, but they will have scant esteem for me.

I was a stranger with Philippe and his peers, too. Where is my homeland? Who are "my own"? A rejected child grows into a rootless adult. But I will find my roots again. I must.

I catch sight of Michel and cry out, "Papa!" He turns toward me. I slide off my perch and run to him.

My father. His head is squarish, with a rough crew cut of graying hair, his jaw is jutting. Yet his blue eyes have a tender glance. He is built like a block of granite. I throw my arms around his neck.

"Well, my girl, what do you think of your own countryside?"

"Smells good."

"When you're less tired, you'll get up at five one morning and we'll walk all the fenced fields."

"Fine. Now take me to see the dovecote?"

Michel frowns. He looks like a peasant counting.

"A good break when that fellow from Paris bought all the beams. That way, I could rebuild the stables."

There it is. He's telling me, in a roundabout way, the results of his sums.

"Have you money troubles, Papa?"

"We are very poor rich people, Céline. We can't sell any of the land because, if we do, there's no more to buy. And the sale of stock brings us barely enough to live on. As for the milk, why bother even to mention it?"

I look at the dovecote once more and think of the royal favorites. "Follies" were built for them at the people's expense: I shan't have my folly.

"Tell me, Papa, is it because of your money worries that you never remarried?"

"It's hard for me to set up a woman in this house, Céline. It belongs to you."

All of a sudden, my childhood image has a crack in it. The father in whose nearness I have sought sanctuary and protection cannot live on my sufferance, more unprovided for than a farmhand: This reality spoils my recollections. Michel is a remembered strength; he cannot live as my dependent.

"If you hadn't been here, Papa, I'd have rented Hérouville. It would no longer be mine. You have kept it and improved it; it belongs to you. Besides, you are my heir!"

This legal fact makes him laugh, but he is touched by it all the same.

Yet I suspect that he regrets not being an "owner." Attachment to the land is our second nature, the basis for our social classifications, and for a great many of us, a reason for living. It is not explicable or subject to discussion—it is an instinct transmitted by the blood. I understand it. Unconsciously, I returned to the source, drawn by the violent joy I feel in contact with "my piece of earth."

"Let me live on here until I die, Céline. I ask no more. I wouldn't be able to get used to any place else."

I embrace Michel with tears in my eyes. This surprises him, for we are not a demonstrative people: He excuses it by thinking that I'm ill.

Shrill voices from the farm courtyard. Auguste is leading Prince from his box toward the van from the cooperative. Prince stamps the ground and raises dust, then spreads his hind legs and voids a huge stream of urine.

"Oh, the dirty bastard! Whenever I get him all sleeked up, he gets himself all muddy . . ."

My father stands admiring this mastodon whose coat ripples like watered silk.

"He's a great, fine male, just the same!"

"Then be nice: give him a real female for a change, not just a sperm catcher," I suggest.

Michel bursts out laughing, and his laugh is good and deep.

"Come on, little girl. Let's go to lunch."

Julie sees us walk up to the house hand in hand. She can't get over it. I go upstairs to fetch a sweater and my bag. My bed is spread open, and the window is thrown wide. She's killing my germs! Ah, well, I know how to be patient. But this time I don't want my patience to be in vain.

After having drunk her frightful coffee with chicory, we leave for Cherbourg. I settle down beside my father and stretch one arm along the back of the seat toward the nape of his neck. We could be taken for a happy couple.

"Why do you want to go to your mother's grave?"

"Posthumous affection. What was she like, Papa?"

"It was so long ago . . ."

"Thirty-one years exactly. Tell me."

"She was nice. She must have had bad memories of the day we made you."

"The day *you* made me . . ."

"Yes. She filled out very fast."

"I was a big baby, and that's why she died. Is that it?"

We are both silent.

I think of that nineteen-year-old child whom my father terrified because he had taken her without gentleness. And I had ripped her apart. Between us, we'd killed her. She left us Hérouville. Perhaps to bring us together. Perhaps to keep us apart. I lower my eyes and forget the landscape as we hurry by. I'd like to buy sheaves of roses. A puerile reaction.

We climb the steep gravel path that leads to the Cherbourg cemetery. My mother's father was a sailor. He had wanted to be buried here. The dead have a grand view over the dry docks. Cherbourg backs up into the great black rock of Roule, and the houses tumble down from it toward the port. This city is like a hunchbacked crab that stretches two claws toward the open sea. Here, when it doesn't rain outright, it either dribbles or mists. If the sky is blue, the wind must be high enough to have swept every cloud from the sky.

I place my flowers on the grave and read: *Céline Lemonnier,* a Céline long since mingled with the earth from which blooms the pink camellias and full-blown mimosa in the spring. We do not tarry. Our dead young woman unites us in a single drive of living egotism. She is no more than a will-o'-the-wisp.

"Are we going to Vauville right away?"

"Yes, I'll take you there, but I'll wait in the car."

We don't say another word.

We take the road to Vauville. The Hague is little known. This slab of upright granite facing the Anglo-Norman islands is a grandiose dolmen towering above the eddies and currents that undermine its base. Jagged rocks form an avant-garde of little pointed islets as sharp as sharks' teeth. The hedge-hopping part of World War II saw the bodies of men torn to pieces on those rocks; never was a June tide so dirty as then. A few blockhouses are still reminders of that grim adventure, and the peasants now use them for storing their hay. The villages are dreary fortresses, fearing bad weather.

My grandmother lives in a low manor house of blue granite. Her hydrangeas screen the windows so that she can see the village only by looking through their great round heads. I ring the bell. I ask myself why my heart's beating so hard. My gesture to go call on her is normal enough. It's as if I had misgivings.

A red-faced servant comes to open the door. Her hips are so wide she could deliver a calf. She is ageless.

"Good morning, madame. I am Céline Lemonnier. I've come to see my grandmother."

"Who's there?"

I hear two high notes, sounding a little alarm of anxiety. My call is an event. I catch sight of white hair behind the hydrangeas.

"It's Céline, the daughter of that Michel Lemonnier."

I go in and up three steps. A miracle happens. I want to reach out to touch her, to fall on my knees, to laugh or cry: my mother's mother is a delightful being who wears around her hair a bandeau of shades of periwinkle and lime blossom. She is not at all like those old farm women who look as dried up as a gnarled thorn brier. She has the laughing face of those who have been subject only to the smaller storms. She is well preserved.

"Céline, my lamb. High time you came to see me. I thought I was going to die without laying eyes on you again."

Die! That's out of the question. My grandmother pleases

me greatly, and without any conscious effort to attract her, I feel myself loved from the start.

"Ah, no, Mamie.* You must go on living, please . . . at least till All Saints' Day."

"I'll try, if you promise to come visit me often. But I'm afraid that wild man of a father of yours won't let you. I saw you so seldom when you were little."

"Papa isn't an unkind wild man. I've known lots worse in Paris!"

And I find my voice breaking as I tell her about my flight from Hérouville, my studies, my marriage, my book, and then Philippe's leaving me, my unhappiness. . . . Mamie weeps, and I do, too, but almost with joy.

"Did Michel Lemonnier go fetch you?"

"Yes, without him I'd have died just from being sick and tired of it all."

We shed a few more tears. My grandmother cries tiny tears that bathe her weary eyes and then run their course down the fine wrinkles of her aged face. We end up blowing our noses at the same time.

"What are your plans now?"

"I'll stay at Hérouville all summer. Then, later on . . ."

"Come often, my lamb. You're at home here. After all, this house will belong to you soon. I have good overseers whom you must learn to take at their true worth. I'll arrange for them to meet you."

"There's plenty of time, dear one."

*Mamie—an appellation of endearment. Roughly, "my dear one."

"*You* have plenty of time, but I don't."

In my mind's eyes, I see the big, red-faced maid and a man of the same stock. They look me over defiantly: I am their future, and peasants look ahead; they fear risk, and to them I am a stranger. I smile. I promise. I smile again, and once more I promise. I kiss my dear one good-by until tomorrow.

"Did you come by car?"

"Yes. My father drove me over. You see how well-intentioned he is!"

I have lied without wanting to.

"Tomorrow I'll hitchhike."

At the door my grandmother's maid tells me, "Madame Céline, Bernard could go pick you up. You shouldn't ride with just anybody."

Who is Bernard who will drive over to fetch me from home tomorrow? I kiss my grandmother once more and run toward Michel. He has been waiting for two hours and is furious.

"You've been crying."

"Think nothing of it: I've found myself a grandmother. I'll come back to see her often. I'm already afraid of losing her."

Michel shuts up tight.

"Drop me off at Cherbourg, Papa. I'd like to buy a few things."

He relaxes and goes with me into the stores. I buy a pair of velours slacks, a fisherman's sou'wester, some cotton knits, and especially licorice sticks, honey candies, and cough drops.

I hesitate before going to replenish my stock of books but enter the bookstore just the same, with a foretaste of morbid enjoyment. There it is. I see Philippe's latest novel. And I behold him again hunched over his typewriter, typing with two fingers. I move toward him silently, bringing him a fresh drink of lemon and mint. It's a mixture of my own invention, and no one else can prepare it for him as I do. Small consolation! He simply enjoys a new taste. When one has loved a man like you, Philippe, it seems impossible to love anyone else.

My throat contracts once more, and I feel it burning away. I need to hunch down in a bed again and pull the sheet up over my head. I'm an ostrich.

"Are you tired, Céline?"

"I'm sleepy. For a first day of convalescence, you'll agree this is a full one! Stop, Papa. Look at that old woman on the soft shoulder."

"Don't you recognize her? That's old Citouenne."

"But isn't she dead?"

"She hasn't stood still long enough to die!"

Citouenne is an image out of my childhood, a little ageless black ant without any family who goes from Valognes to Cherbourg on foot three times a week to sell a basketful of apples or a dozen pears, according to the season. The town council gives her welfare, but Citouenne has kept her pilgrim's staff. She is in the image of our countryside, tenacious, striking a hard bargain, fiercely independent. We roll along slowly until we are abreast of her. She does not look up. She is bent toward the ground whose every crack she knows by heart.

"Last winter, I picked her up one day. I thought I'd be asphyxiated. She hadn't washed since the 1914 war!"

"What about the 'Marquis and Marquise des Grèves'? Are they still alive?"

"Yes, you'll see them if you go with me some day to Crasvill-erie. They drank up all their war damages, and now they live in a blockhouse at Landemer. They once owned one of the most beautiful farms in this part of the country."

I remember those two tattered ghosts clinging together and supporting each other's faltering footsteps. In their fall, they had preserved such a bearing that the whole countryside called them "the marquisses." On June 6 at daybreak, a man-of-war had picked out their manor house for target practice. Miraculously their cellars escaped, and the proprietors drank to the miracle. When the government awarded them meager damages, they drank to their memories.

"How do they manage for food?"

"Certain old ladies of the landed gentry hereabouts still prepare a 'stew for their poor' once a week. The marquisses go from one chateau to another and from one stew to another. Alcoholics don't eat much."

"I know."

We reach Hérouville in time for dinner.

Philippe has not telephoned. My health does not matter to him. After dinner, I go straight to bed. The happy impressions I have garnered since my return are muddled in my head. The harshest trial for a woman is to be blotted out, no longer to be anything. I was a shade in Philippe's life, but at least a familiar shade. Does he still remember at least that I exist? My grandmother Phellie would perhaps have thrown a pair of boots at his head. Or would she have turned into a ghost, as I did? Or ended her love by turning it into hate?

I listen to the silence of the farm for a long time, and then go to sleep.

Michel knocks on the door to waken me. I slept straight through, but my sleep was troubled and heavy with anxiety. My throat starts to tighten up, and Michel quickly stuffs my morning ration of honey into me. He is attention itself, but I wish he'd go away again. I am humiliated, and my sugary cough makes me feel ill. I get myself under control. Julie comes in, carrying her tray of food. Habits are essential to her: Since she served us this way yesterday, it will be the same every day, and the least change will be a source of real distress for her.

"I bought you some honey from the Brick Gulf area. The bees there feed on the broom around Fermanville. It's easier on your throat," she says.

She has put the best face possible on her capitulation. I will gratefully cough my morning cough scented with broom.

Michel cuts his omelet into big bites. He is wearing a sea-blue turtleneck that sets off his graying hair.

"My, you're handsome this morning, Papa."

"Think so?" He sounds almost worried and quickly adds, "There's a meeting of the town council."

How badly he lies.

"I'd like us to be very good friends, Papa."

"I'd like that, too, Céline."

"Then let me tell you something. I've lived for five years beside a man who is a master liar. You lie badly."

Michel blows up. I hand him the honey pot.

"I forbid you to pass judgment on my private life."

"Promise, word of honor! Given your sporty attire, I suppose you have a date with a young woman. That means you're in good health."

Michel is amazed. How has this man been able to live so completely alone, spied on by a whole small town, hiding his joys without being able to share them with anybody?

I throw my arms around him.

"I'm glad for you, but if you don't come home at all tonight, I'll go to the police to report that someone has kidnaped my father."

"I'll pick you up at six o'clock at your grandmother's."

"Don't bother. It's out of your way."

"It's right *on* my way."

So, my father doesn't play games within the town limits!

He is a very lively fellow when he leaves, and for a moment I feel a little downcast. She's a lucky young woman. She is desired, and Michel is happy. . . . For that, I'd like to thank her. But let them keep their lovemaking in another place, not Hérouville.

Will Philippe come to see me at least once? If he comes, he'll greet me as usual: "Hello, you! You're not in very good shape." Why does one always grow weary? How is it that laws that have kept a city on its feet fall into desuetude? Why does everything wear out? I dream of things that endure. I hear Michel start his car. This departure brings to mind other departures. My father and my husband are alike—why did I never see their similarities? Is Michel as inconstant in love? Probably. But his flirtations amuse and reassure me while Philippe's crucified me. Like Philippe, my father lightly skims the surface of his responsibilities rather than facing them head on. And he, too, is afraid of cluttering up his life. The day Philippe stopped loving me, had I been self-effacing and conciliatory enough, he and I would have turned into one of those couples that abound, a façade with nothing behind it. But I could not compromise. Now I must not hamper Michel's freedom. But there is a tie that binds us: Hérouville. I get up, feeling smothered, imprisoned between two men who at the moment don't have me on their minds at all.

To amuse myself, I try on yesterday's purchases. I bought a pair of orange velours slacks. I scarcely dare look at myself; my wan face cuts me to the quick. I understand Philippe's coldness: Who could want a woman as washed out as I am?

I go out, searching for an out-of-the-way hedge. The grass is tall. Next month they'll mow the hay, and the least shower will bathe the countryside with the heady perfume that foretells summer storms and later on the equinox. The earth exults, the sea tides change, and the great waves of June water the salt meadows. I am a creature of earth. I love my land, its smells, it scars, its seasons. I know its herbs like an old woman who collects her simples. I lie down now on my back, my arms close to my body, my hands flat on the ground, in the very position I will be given the day I enter into my eternity of mingling with this earth, becoming flowering grasses such as these on which my animals slowly chew their cud.

When I go back to the house for lunch, Julie serves me a large, overcooked steak and cottage cheese. As soon as the first warm days appear, our farms give off the slightly tart odor of milk that has turned in the sun and then been drained carefully in fine linen. A motor rumbles softly in the farm courtyard. Julie casts a wary eye outside.

"It's the son of your grandmother's overseer, the one from Herquemoulin. He goes to college to become a teacher."

I get up from table to welcome this elite member of society. I encounter a Viking. Ah, what a handsome young man! Scrunched down on my flat heels, I raise my head. I smile, I thank him effusively for having gone to the trouble. . . . I offer him a cup of coffee. I put sugar in it. I have lived up to my ears in slick talkers these last years, and his shyness surprises me. Het gets around to telling me that he has just finished Normal School. We leave for my grandmother's. I can't detach my eyes from his sunbleached hair, his smooth skin that one would expect to find beardless. Bernard is an easy-going young man; by his side, one's body and mind are at ease. I'm still looking at him. He does not compare with Michel or Philippe. I smile at an over-age adolescent whom I would like to kiss because he smells as pleasant as my earth does at the hour Michel gets up.

We talk about teaching, about Camus. He is our "open sesame." Bernard relaxes, quotes passages from *The Stranger.* I know Algiers, tell him about the rocks of Tipaza, about the waterless land, the burning sand, the ink-dark sea so hot and salty that I floated in it with my belly to the sun.

"If you try the temperature of the water around here—I took my first swim of the season yesterday—you'll find it's like melted ice."

"I'd like to take a swim, but I'm afraid I'd get sick."

"I'll go with you."

This man-child has a protective tone. This comforts me, for I was afraid he took me for an old woman.

"I'd also like to visit grandmother's salt marshes."

He scowls. I understand quickly that I must efface all impression of being a landowner visiting her acres escorted by the overseer or, in this case, his son.

"I feel an intense physical joy in rediscovering these vast open spaces, the wind, the moors, the marshes. For five years, I was a prisoner in an apartment which hadn't a single window that opened on a tree. It's no wonder I have hunger pains!"

"Your father wants to raise sheep."

"He'll have to, otherwise he'll soon be bankrupt."

I am poor. Bernard smiles. We reach Vauville. My dear grandmother is waiting.

"Good-by, madame. Would you like me to call for you tomorrow?"

"Call me Céline, or I'll think I'm an old woman."

He laughs. He is a creature hewn of alabaster. His personality is unfinished and vulnerable. Everything must make an impression on him. I hesitate. I know my own desperate need to be loved. I smile at him. I want to think only of myself. After all, he was a happy child. I was not.

"Come early and we'll go and swim. I'll try to be brave."

"See you tomorrow, Céline."

Mamie appears once more. We laugh. We open cupboards and count the sweet-smelling old sheets. I make tea, being careful not to make it so strong as to give her palpitations. I raise my head at the least sound. Bernard can't be far off, and I'd be happy to go and play with him.

At five o'clock Michel calls for me. He stands there stiffly. My grandmother hesitates, then smiles at him. I lean toward her and kiss her three times.

"Till tomorrow, dear one. Bernard said he'd pick me up."

"He's a good child."

"Yes, I find him most accommodating."

I look Michel over. I don't dare ask him if he has had a happy afternoon. Just the same, I try.

"Have you spent your time happily, Papa?"

"Yes, but I'm worried. My back aches. Last winter I had lumbago, and I'm afraid I'll have it again. It's tough to grow old."

"You're not even remotely old! And if you were not my father, I'd be very much attracted by your charm."

"Oh, I'm old all right."

He is dead set, and suddenly his mouth draws taut: He is in pain.

"Let's stop at Valognes for me to buy a tube of ointment to rub you with."

"Oh, come on, Céline!"

"Come on, what? Why should it upset me? Yours isn't the first male back I've seen in my life."

I play the worldly-wise, yet aside from Philippe . . .

"Buy your ointment in Cherbourg. The pharmacist at Valognes is a town councillor, and the whole countryside will know my lumbago has started up again."

Michel is like one of those racing dogs who has been whipped. His day can't have been a mad success.

I buy my ointment and some painkiller. I don't dare to help him out of the car, but he makes a wry face. He eats his dinner fast and then goes up to bed. Our rooms are separated by a tiny, dark room that houses a collection of old white iron-stone pots.

I knock on his door. I ask myself how often have I entered

my father's bedroom. It is furnished without taste, my mother having changed nothing about the bedroom of her mother. Thus we live among the horrors accumulated by generations who wished to economize. Only our wardrobes are ornamented with carving and as vast as caverns. I remember having hidden in them often when I was a child.

Michel is lying on his stomach.

"Does it hurt?"

"Yes, worse and worse."

I raised his pajama jacket and lower the pants. My father has a body as broad as a boat. I place the palms of my hands on his warm flesh, and his powerful muscles contract under my fingers. I begin to massage the hollow of his back just above the kidneys. We do not dare talk. I am moved. I work hard at it. Rarely have I known as powerfully male an odor as that given off by Michel's skin. After a while I stop massaging. I can scarcely lift a finger. I help him turn over. The pain is sometimes so great that his face turns white.

"I'm going downstairs to phone the doctor."

"No. It will go away."

I go to get a glass of water and bump into Julie.

"My father's in pain, Julie."

"Give him a little glass of calvà. That'll put him on his feet again."

Calvados is our cure-all. It kills worms, makes labor pains bearable, takes care of lumbago; we even give a taste to rabbits before we draw them.

Julie hands me the fat-bellied bottle and a glass. I give Michel a painkiller pill and a glass of alcohol full to the brim. The smell gets to me, envelops me. I look at my father.

"I'll take just a thimbleful with you."

"Don't drink any more than that, Céline."

He doesn't dare check on me, and so I cheat a little. My throat catches fire, and the burning liquid knots my stomach. Soon my head feels flushed, too, and I look forward to the calm that follows this warmth. I would like a second drink.

I lean back against Michel's pillow.

"Go to bed, little Céline. You're a good nurse."

"No, I'll stay up until your pain has calmed down."

The alcohol has numbed us both. We stay there, head against head, with a single wish to be together.

"I'm so pleased to have a big daughter."

"I'm so happy to be with you."

"Don't you find me too much of a . . . peasant?"

"Yes, like one of La Varende's characters."

"D'you like La Varende's books?"

"Yes."

"I've read him. Barbey d'Aurevilly, too."

"I like him better than La Varende."

We talk in low tones, as if telling secrets. I look at Michel with his head crushing the pillow. There's nothing about him of the intellectual undermined by despair. He is characteristic of that type of countryman shaped by nature in her own likeness. Like nature itself, he is ageless.

This evening he is just my father, and the pereceptivity of his mind is worth all the empty knowledge of those degree-laden fools who have cluttered up my life these past few years. I run my hand over his hair.

"I also read whatever I can lay my hands on about Napoleon."

I wish he would leave off this inventory of his reading, it humiliates him and disturbs our intimacy.

"Does it still hurt?"

"No, so long as I don't move a muscle."

"I'll massage you again in the morning. Don't get up. We'll have our *collation* in your room."

I feel sweet and warm. The alcohol has made me happy. I'm sleepy. I close my eyes.

I wake up at six in the morning because Michel has stirred. We slept leaning against each other, he numbed by his pain-killer, I soothed by the Calvados.

"Céline, did you sleep . . . in here?"

"Yes, I won't even have to get dressed. It's all done."

We are so surprised to wake up like this that we start to laugh. I begin to cough. My fingers tighten around Michel's arm. I hide my head against his shoulder. At this moment he is the refuge I so often regretted he was not. He holds me to him as if he wanted to absorb my coughing fits.

"Did you drink last evening, Céline?"

"A little."

"Why do you like alcohol?"

"It's not that I like alcohol, Papa; I like its effect. It reassures my uncertainties. I draw enough courage from it to be able to face others without the immediate fear that they are hostile to me."

"Are you afraid of living?"

"Certainly. But I don't have that fear at Hérouville."

"Nothing's to stop your living here the greater part of the year. Your husband wants a divorce . . ."

Michel's bed becomes an abyss. I knew that Philippe would leave me. I did not know he was unmanly enough to warn my father so that he might avoid any unpleasant action on my part.

"Papa, why doesn't he love me any longer? He loved me once."

"Because love passes, little Céline; a woman soon ceases to hold any surprises. Eat lentils every day and you'll throw up at the mere smell of them."

"What did he say to you when you came to get me?"

"Oh, phrases. Your husband is quite a talker."

It's as well not to know. Hérouville is all around us. I slept huddled against Michel, the rising sun drinks in the dew on our pasture lands, the cows have been milked, Prince bellows for his feed, which seems to him slow in coming. My dear grand-mother is waking up now and will await me. Bernard is still asleep.

"I'll go down and make your coffee, Papa."

"Don't tell Julie you slept . . ."

"Certainly not!"

Julie gets down the coffeepot.

"You are a proper sight!"

"I didn't sleep well. I was worried about my father."

"Well, if he didn't run around like a young man! And at his age, too."

"He's not old, Julie. And he's not a monk."

"Who'll look out for your interests if a woman comes and sets up her children here?"

"No one will come, Julie, and Hérouville belongs to my father."

"No. It comes from your mother's side and it's rightfully yours. Instead of marrying some old fellow in Paris, you should have taken one of the fine lads from around here. He'd have brought his own settlement, and you could have set up the biggest farm in the whole Cotentin peninsula."

Julie has let fly all her regrets at one clip. She hasn't said as many words since last Michaelmas, the day on which rents and tenant farmers' accounts are due throughout the countryside, and tongues are loosed.

"Make us some *good* coffee, Julie."

"With the chicory added, it's good for your health."

"I'll feed it to Prince."

"Make it yourself since I make it so bad!"

"Julie, don't give me apoplexy. I'm like my grandmother Phellie."

"Why, so you are, at that! Then I hope you stay on at Hérouville and look after your interests."

I wonder whether or not Michel has some bastard child living in the neighborhood. Julie's harping worries me. I look at her. She has frugal ways. From one All Saints' Day to the next, she is dressed in black. Her only domain is this high-ceilinged kitchen with its many copper utensils that reflect my image in russet. Michel has bought a huge refrigerator into which she plunges half her thin body to retrieve an earthenware crock of butter. How can one grow attached to such little things?

"At my age, Céline, I'm too old to change my ways." She bows her ferret face as if she were admitting a secret.

I understand. Her refuge is in that bundle of habits that go to make up a life. She does, indeed, plunge completely into her refrigerator from which she retrieves things endlessly.

I take another look at myself in her gleaming copper casseroles. How much I'd like my looks if my cheeks were filled out like that, my hair a Venetian red, my skin golden. And certainly Philippe would love me then.

"What time does Léon come?"

"When he's finished drinking."

From eight o'clock on, Hérouville and its environs wait for Léon. A great friend of Auguste, Léon has been our postman for thirty years. He belongs to our mornings as much as do the Cooperative's milk truck and the baker's cart. But Léon keeps us waiting. He has his stops between the post office and ourselves, and they're always the same. He is the only one in the entire countryside who missed the Normandy landings. His fright at the first bombardments was so great that he drank a half bottle of the local brandy in a single draught. Léon lived out that historic day passed out on a heap of green underbrush in a ditch by the woods of Octeville. The noise did not even wake him. He is as brittle and blackened as an apple branch in December. Alcohol has fairly eaten away his flesh, shrunken his stomach, washed out his eyes. Léon is a sleepwalker whose first calvà of the day wakes him and whose last lays him out cold.

Perhaps some day he'll bring me a letter from Philippe. Or he'll give it to our neighbor Letellier by mistake. In that case, I'll never receive it. I take up the coffee. Michel grunts whenever he changes the position of his lower back.

"It's going to rain. Are you going to Vauville just the same?"

"Yes."

"I wish you'd get up earlier. It would work if you'd go to bed earlier. Just don't stay too late at Vauville, that's all."

I belong to my father. He puts up with sharing me provided it's on a strictly equitable basis. He expects to be cheated of his share in advance. . . .

He hawks and spits. I feel let down. I need to raise my face to that manna we draw from the skies in all seasons. I leave Michel to his *Memories of Saint Helena*. Mindful of Julie, I throw back my bed covers and rumple my bed. Then I put on my sou'wester.

When I go out, I greet Prince. Auguste is asleep, huddled in the loose hay. The great bull looks me over and bellows. As if by some miracle, he raises his hoofs each time they touch the limp body stretched out beneath them. How many times has Prince drenched old Auguste with a flood of urine?

I don't go far. My horizons are drawn in today. Hérouville is solitary, and our nearest neighbor, Letellier, is nearly two miles away, hidden behind a dozen hedges. I come across only the butcher driving his little delivery truck from one farm to the next. I smile at him, and he hesitates to return my smile. He decides simply to nod his head in my direction. It's strange how the natives of Normandy always seem to be looking out from behind a peephole.

I lean against my favorite rail fence. Life is simple when it goes by this way, scarcely touching me. Is this peace, at last? No, peace can't be simply a withdrawal from everything. It must be the acceptance of everything. I don't want to delude myself. I am just beginning to experience a little quietude. If Philippe were dead, I would be a calm and quiet widow.

Bernard comes to fetch me in the early afternoon. He has a slight cough, so we don't go swimming. I greet my grandmother with a kiss, throw my arms around her, smooth her hair.

"I love you, dear one. I love you, I love you."

"How you do need to say it, my lamb!"

"If you only knew . . . There's nothing more stifling than words of love suppressed because one has no one to tell them to or because the person to whom they'd be spoken would hear them with indifference or impatience. Once upon a time, I was made ridiculous by love—I can't think of anything worse, my dear one. Now I've found you, don't leave me, don't abandon me for any reason whatsoever!"

"I'm deeply at fault, Céline. I should have faced your father years ago and asked for your custody when you were a child. But the women of my generation were brought up to respect men's decisions."

"D'you think Michel loves me?"

"It's hard for me to tell . . . You are intelligent; perhaps too intelligent. Love does not reason why. You see, love gives and does not wait to receive first. It is also, sometimes, a question of taming a person, winning him over . . ." And she goes on telling me about the nature of love. I listen with half-shut eyes. I see a young woman, small, slender-waisted, tiny feet bound in kidskin shoes, a little veil lifted by fingertips revealing a wide, blue gaze. A young woman, the object of much fulsome praise.

"For example," she goes on, "you laugh badly. When you laugh, you choke and cry. You don't raise your chin. Laughter is a very important part of seduction! Look at me. Straighten up. There now, raise your chin, more, now laugh!"

Her index finger raises my chin and I, who scarcely know how to smile, laugh in the angels' faces. She shrugs. I am the despair of my grandmother.

Ogdensburg Public Library
Ogdensburg, New York

And so the days roll by without shocks. I don't count them. What would be the point? I have stopped waiting.

My land has recognized one of its own and taken me back. It pours its strength into me, unties my tensions, calms my revolts. I am almost serene, even though I think I'm living without a goal.

I get up at dawn without effort and go with Michel across the fenced pasture lands still damp with dew. We hold hands. I hang onto him in order to disengage from a tangled clump of buttercups and daisies. I've always tried to avoid crushing flowers. Michel recognizes this trait in me, and his tenderness could quickly become tyranny. He takes the adoration I give my grandmother very ill indeed.

Sometimes we go beyond the Barnavast woods and wander as far as the banks of the Saire where my father goes trout fishing. I sit on a stump, and my thoughts quiet down, losing themselves in the meanderings of the river. I have the simultaneous impression of emptying myself of everything and of bathing in renewal.

I go to Vauville every afternoon. By mutual consent Bernard and I have started making repairs and improvements about the house. We give the exposed beams a coat of flat varnish. We repaint the shutters. We plan to clean up the attic. Can it be that we want to be together? We find this work an easy pretext. One morning the sun at last appears. I trot along beside Michel, finally free of my sou'wester. My father smiles: Four days of dry weather will let him get in the hay without danger of having it rot in the barns. The whole countryside is raising its head, sniffing the wind, fearing the shifting of the tide, making calculations. The *Channel Almanac* announces: possible rain. And the old people say, "Let whoever wants to lie talk about the weather."

Finally, Léon brings me a letter. Philippe is back after three weeks in the States. He writes me news of our friends there. For me, Americans had been those big blond fellows who gave me chewing gum in our town in the Place de Sainte-Mère-Eglise. When Phillipe and I visited their country, I found it to be far less light-hearted. He was amused at my disabused reaction. Now he plans to go to Deauville in August and would like to see me. I can guess the subject of our next meeting. I throw out this letter that hasn't the least expression of tenderness in it.

Bernard calls for me early.

"Céline, let's go for a swim."

"Fine idea."

I need violent action to forget Philippe's letter.

My dear grandmother lets me go but with misgivings. She gives me enormous bath towels embroidered with her initials. Bernard chooses to go to the Calvary-of-the-Dunes.

A huge calvary dominates a sandy moor that rises and falls and is finally lost at one end of the tip of Jobourg and on the other at Sionville. Great numbers of sheep without a shepherd graze there on the stubble and drink the rainwater that collects in holes. The moor pivots on the axis of Vauville, and the ewe who might wander beyond the confines of this permitted range finds herself rolling down the incline that ends in the hard sand of the beach. At our feet, the gray-blue waves assault the sand. And in this fierce war the sea slowly wins.

I turn my head away when Bernard drops his blue jeans. We

tear off our clothes as if they were fetters. I turn around. He is ready. He has the body of an adolescent. I think of Michel's massive body.

"Come, Céline, give me your hand. The path isn't easy."

We cache our clothes and he rolls up the towels. We are awkward with each other. I should have worn a less revealing bathing suit. My attention is riveted on the path, and I place my feet on the bias in order not to slide. As soon as we reach the beach, we are seized by the immensity and solitude. We seem like two dwarfs who mark the cold and humid shore with their narrow tread. The sea washes away our footprints with a sound of suction. Suddenly anxious, I press my companion's fingers. As far as the horizon, the flat beach runs its yellow ribbon that gradually narrows until it mingles with the gray-blue sky.

"You have to run in, Céline. And be sure you don't hesitate before you throw yourself into the water."

He pulls me along. I'm running, and the waves are drawing near. Bernard pauses a second, then runs even faster. I cry out. My body feels as if slashed with a thousand razor cuts. I lose my breath. I want to cry out again. I'm being cut down, asphyxiated. I am the victim of violent blows, and the water plunges down my throat. My eyes burn. A strong hand encircles my neck and lifts my head. I come up and open my mouth like a little carp. Air filters into my lungs between two furrows of salt. Another hand raises me up. Suddenly I melt; my body becomes another young, supple body, my blood is like quicksilver carrying my well-being along in its headlong flow. I open happy eyes on the horizon, the sky, the white blots of the sheep grazing beneath the Cross on the Dunes. I am young and the world is young, too.

Bernard is near me, his hair like that of a wet puppy. He continues holding me up.

"Let's go farther out."

"No, I'm afraid of the current."

He laughs at my fear and opens his wake to my advance. I follow him, docile, my energy restored. I swim fast. Suddenly my fingers stiffen. I turn about. The beach seems so far away. My strokes are hurried, my movements no longer well-coordinated. My breath comes in gasps. Finally, I reach the beach, exhausted, breathless, thrown down on the greenish slime, a mixture of sea grasses and empty shells left by the last great wave. During that eternity of a few seconds in which panic took over my will, I had called for Philippe. Now I would like to drown him.

Bernard comes to join me.

"Feel tired?"

"Yes. Go ahead without me."

"I'm a little winded, too."

He stretches out. The water slips beneath our backs and raises us. We float like two empty shells. A stronger wave than the last throws me against him farther up on the strand.

"Who can see us?"

"The sheep, if they're not nearsighted, and the gulls who may take us for fish thrown up on the sand."

My companion's face has changed. He is tense now. It's I who kiss him, his cool, salty lips that soon grow warm.

"Céline."

"Shhh!"

How long is it since anyone has wanted me like this? What does it matter? The past disgusts me; only the present moment interests me. We let ourselves be guided by instinct. At first, he does not dare to touch me—then he makes love to me like a tornado. My body is thrust deeply into the sand, kneaded by another, a violent body, and when Bernard utters a groan I don't know if it is his or mine . . . or that of the wind's echo. He throws his head back on the sand; his *sexe* is the same rose-violet as the foxglove that blooms along our hedgerows. Our bathing suits float, abandoned, on the rising tide. He gets up and pulls me along with him into the water.

"The sun's low. It must be late, Bernard. My father will worry."

"Your father doesn't like me, Céline. Do you know why?"

"I can't fathom it. He ignored my existence for thirty years, and now he's discovered me. Is it guilt or surpirse? He has the reactions of a peasant who now locks up something of value he'd misplaced."

"Will you come back tomorrow?"

"It's Sunday. Come to fetch me Monday and pick me up by the pasture where the calves are put out to grass. I don't want any scenes between my father and you."

"Perhaps he thinks the son of a sharecropper isn't a fit companion."

"Now there you're completely off the track. There isn't a more liberal or unconventional man than Michel!"

This youngster has managed to irritate me. What right has he to pass judgment on my father?

"Let's go and get dressed."

He looks unhappy. I kiss him. He smiles, and we run for the dunes. We share one more embrace. I feel as if I were asking him to forgive me. We dress quickly.

I give my grandmother a quick hug in passing, and a little

after seven, we reach Hérouville. My hair is still damp, my slacks are full of sand. I look as if I'd been shipwrecked.

"Where've you been?"

"I went for a swim."

Julie raises her eyes to heaven and rushes to get me a bowl of steaming hot soup.

"Go change your clothes, Céline. You'll catch cold. What a crazy idea to go swimming in water as cold as the Channel!"

"I love the sea, and I had a fine swim."

My father doesn't understand me. The people from this region are of two different species: the peasants, and the fishermen. Those who work the land hate the sea and despise the fishermen who seem to them but poor earners. The fishermen more than despise—they spit on—the peasants bound to the earth and to a life without danger. In the coastal villages, the municipal councils are always divided into two hostile blocks. Neither side ever wins.

All through dinner Michel keeps his eye on me. He noses me out.

"Tell me what kind of day you have had."

"I called on *grand-mère*, and I went for a swim."

"With your chauffeur?"

"Yes."

"Remember that in our part of the country the hedges have eyes and ears."

"What kind of story do you want people to invent? Our province has changed. It was torn apart by the Landing, by the Allied boys who fell from the sky and killed our witches. Now we have tourists instead. The peasants look at television, Papa, and wait for the dates when their subsidies are due from the

Department of Agriculture. Come, Papa, the day of the ladies with the green hats is over!"

Michel does not believe me.

He remembers the local refrain: "A certain person told me . . ." or, "I let someone sound off. . . ." Valognes has long been a little town of closed shutters where each street crossing had its pitiless peek-a-boo artist. But the old women have died off carrying their spleen back to the devil. The young couldn't care less. I look at my father tenderly. It took unusual courage and also a degree of distance from Hérouville to lead any kind of personal love life. He reminds me of an old gossip whom he had once forced to take a ducking in the public baths for her lies. But people say so many things. . . .

"Papa, tomorrow's Sunday. Let's go out like a couple of lovers. I'd like so much to visit Tourlaville."

"I don't think I can . . ."

"Break your date."

He lowers his head.

"It's hard. We've spent Sundays together for the past twenty years."

"So this isn't the light-o'-love of the other afternoon?"

"No. This is an old relationship. I always feel responsible for the women who . . . love me."

"Responsible? Or weighed down by?"

"Both. I hate to break off."

"So you try to temporize?"

"Yes. But in these parts, everyone ends up by knowing everything."

"Papa, for one Sunday out of so many, she won't say a word. Stay and spend the day with me?"

"She would like to meet you."

He tries to be conciliating.

"No. Do whatever you wish outside of Hérouville, but here it's our home for the two of us. I need peace. Hérouville and you are enough to make me happy."

I've won. Michel stretches out his legs in front of the television and I sit on the floor with my head thrown back against his thigh. He falls asleep. I am happy. I'd like a glass of *calvà* to "set" my happiness so that I wouldn't know any longer whether it was against Philippe's leg or my father's I was leaning.

I get up softly.

"Are you drinking, Céline?"

Michel is on his feet. I should have remembered that a peasant sleeps with one eye open. He leans out and waters the hydrangeas with alcohol, *calvà* the color of old gold.

"I didn't slap you when you were a child; don't force me to do it now. Let's go to bed."

The telephone rings.

"Who is it at this hour! Either there's a fire at the town hall or your grandmother is dead."

Michel says this is a neutral voice. As for me, I am suddenly a child with weak legs. It is he who picks up the phone.

"Worse than that! Your husband is fishing for news."

He hands me the phone as if it were a holy water sprinkler. I am the corpse. Philippe's voice is as natural as if he had left me the day before. Does he want to cut short any of my likely complaints? Have I inflicted so many reproaches on him in the past?

He wishes to write a script from my book. I have unlimited confidence in Philippe. He always took care of my interests, and near him I lose that bitterness that makes me consider my interlocutor an adversary.

"You are perhaps too tired to come to Paris?"

Leave my native soil, confine myself, fascinated by Philippe, helpless. . . .

"I feel much better."

"You must start working again. Your last book was good. Are you working on a new one?"

"Yes, I'm well on the way," I lie through my teeth, choked.

"Do you want me to come and see you?"

"Yes. I would prefer that."

We are two like tightrope walkers, counting out our words, edging along.

"I'll see you at my grandmother's at Vauville."

"Don't bother her."

"But you must come to Mamie's. She is an adorable person, and very attractive, like a character in a novel. She looks like a Saxe porcelain cup with a blue silk bow around it."

Philippe laughs. I was witty. It was about time!

"So, see you Saturday; we'll meet at Cherbourg?"

"Yes, I'll meet the morning train."

"Right! See you Saturday, Céline."

"See you soon Philippe."

All that had kept me together collapsed.

I stretch out my hand, reaching for Michel. He is there. And I cry.

"For Christ's sake, Céline, don't be your mother's daughter, be mine! React. If you've been crying for five years in front of your husband, he's been patient; as for me, I would not have endured it! Napoleon jumped on a horse and never came back, and Barbey poisoned his mourner. Give him tit for tat, but don't cry!"

Michel's face has the same disgusted expression it had this morning when he saw me coughing. He shakes me, he bruises me, he thrashes me. What annoys him so much? The flabby human being in front of him? This intruder who comes between us and to whom I give so much consideration? But, dear God, I am not a pyramid. I am a woman, I didn't collapse all by myself. Phillipe pushed me!

"On what grounds do you want to force a man to love you? He loved you. He doesn't love you any more. So, break a soup tureen over his head and leave him, but don't whine. You keep on reciting your misery like a bigot telling her rosary beads."

This time it's too much! Rustic and boorish words are close to my lips. What does he know about love? Love, which—when it goes—digs a precipice, annihilates life, paints the outlines of a familiar décor gray. But what do they have in place of a heart, those men who destroy us, hoping to be spared the sight of a distressed face?

"Wait for him at the ready, this *horsain*.* That reminds me, Monday we cut the hay; go spend a couple of days in Vauville. See you tomorrow, duckie; you might as well sleep."

He turns his back on me.

I go to bed, stunned. I am cold because I have eight hours of solitude ahead of me before dawn. Eight hours of "why," and I've had those so often. Philippe is near. I repeat our words one by one. I make a mistake and start all over again. . . .

Yes, I hated him. But who was duped? I. Philippe was

---

* Expression peculiar to Normandy; not translatable.

shocked, then irritated, then indifferent. Who has been bruised? I. I stoked my resentment like a forge, and every time that Philippe offended me, I congratulated myself on being shrewd enough to hate him. Hatred. Is it possible that it has been my constant companion. There is a kinship for "those who hate." Their solitary rage rocks them with the illusion that hatred is a power raising its followers above the common people. There is a kind of enjoyment in hating well. It is only the exasperation of the badly loved. It enslaves, isolates, consumes. It makes us perfect egoists.

I have been at Hérouville for only a few weeks, and I think less about that necessity to suffer that was my one preoccupation.

I breathe, I cut flowers. I make love to Bernard. I don't hurry any more, in my waking consciousness of the morning, to tell myself at once: I am unhappy.

In this maze that is a woman's love, suffering quickly becomes a first-class mate. We have a taste for long moody enjoyments. How could I stand there calmly when they said of me: "And how is Céline? Still depressed?" I suddenly hate my past weakness. It is only a shameful disease that tarnishes my body.

The failure resembled a victory when fought, but the carelessness of victories often brings us back to failure. As for me, I have only known abdication.

See Philippe again. No. I won't hammer my brain with these two words. I will say to him. . . . No! I won't prepare any dialogue, those long-thought words that one wants to place at any cost and that always fall flat. I will try to be serene. Above all, I won't be bitter.

I will utter banalities. I will ask him to tell me about his next book or his last trip to America.

My bed is mussed and crumpled when I go to sleep at last, numb with good resolutions. Julie, coming back from the seven o'clock mass, brings me my coffee.

"Where is Daddy, Julie?"

"He has gone out, like every other Sunday."

"Where is he going?"

"It's a cousin on your mother's side. I don't like her. She'd like to fart over the top of her head, you know! She has rented her land and plays the lady, but she can't carry it off. She is waiting for her hour, while he chases the young girls. Eventually he will get old, too."

A lowing breaks the silence of Hérouville.

"But that's Prince!"

"Something's wrong and just when your father is not here! It had to happen one day—things have been going too well."

"Shut up and let's go down and see."

I pull on my slacks. Prince lows again, this time with rage. We run to the box stall. And we back up horrified.

"Oh, Julie, and Daddy not back!"

"This had to finish this way! And the farrier is on his Sunday off. As if there were any Sundays for animals!"

Instinctively we move closer together. Our eyes are focused on a pile of blood-stained rags that the beast still avoids. But the smell of blood exasperates Prince. He sees us. He stamps the ground with his right hoof, wheels round, pisses like a fire hose, then, in his rage, starts trampling on the body lying under him.

"Julie, we must do something, maybe Auguste is not dead.

He must have thrown up some blood, alcoholics do that sometimes in the morning."

She doesn't listen. Eyes front, she stares. Does she experience a kind of peasant enjoyment in the face of any violent sight? I don't know. She insults my father with the most vile words. The master is not here; he spent the night with a trollop. Where does it come from, all that filth? I can't stand any more of the soft-sounding blows on the lifeless body or the poisonous litanies. Quickly, as I've often seen it done, I mix some flour in a bucket. I hang the bucket on the end of a long pitchfork and, stiff with fear, I half-open the stall door. In his drunkenness the day before, Auguste didn't chain up Prince properly. He left the chain too loose, and the bull is able to get out of the stall. He is hungry. I know it. Creeping, I push the full bucket far in front of me. Prince never looked so monstrous to me. He buries his enormous head in the mixture, gulps it down, stamps fuming and overturns the bucket, then recovers what he can of the meager pittance. I lie on my stomach and catch Auguste by one of his feet. This dead weight seems heavy. I drag him toward me slowly. Why doesn't Prince charge me? Every morning at this hour somebody cleans his stall and changes his stable litter. But he is fighting with his bucket as it rolls away. He ignores me.

At last I am out, pulling these rags, so soaked in blood they no longer look human. I take his pulse, it is still beating.

"When your father finds out that I let you do this . . . I'm sure he'll want to strangle me!"

"And that won't be any great loss. Instead of muttering insults, it would be better if you'd help me."

Julie looks like a corpse. At this instant Michel comes back from his amorous escapade. He looks at the two of us: I am covered with liquid manure and blood; Julie is the soul of reprobation; Michel sees the outstretched body.

"Call a doctor, Daddy, he's still alive!"

Michel says nothing, he goes toward Prince's box.

"Good God, Céline, you forgot the pitchfork!"

It's his only commentary. Julie flees to the kitchen. I try to call Doctor Carpentier. I am not able to reach him. I feel nauseated. Here, you must not be sick on a Sunday morning. Either the doctor is a bigot and attending High Mass or he is a freethinker and fishing off shore.

"Go and wash yourself, my girl."

Michel takes the phone from my hand. I am sickened. Endlessly I splash myself with icy water. The ambulance from Valognes arrives to take Auguste away. Is he still alive? Who cares about his death? Michel, perhaps, because you can no longer find anyone good at tending bulls.

My father brings me a full pot of coffee. The hot liquid perks me up.

"Get dressed, Céline, and let's get out of here."

I encounter Julie, sepulchral looking in her black clothes, her hands resting flat on her skirt. I shiver, I think of the priestess Pythia or the image of Destiny. . . . From what depths did she pull out those words of hatred she spat out, haggard, lost in the vision of a nightmare in which neither Auguste nor myself had any part? How old can she be? Fifty-five, sixty years old? Michel himself is fifty-one. This house, closed to everybody else, how was it formerly? What happened here after my mother's death?

"How is Auguste?"

"Carpentier says that he vomited two pints of blood at least; he kept him in the hospital. Prince had broken two of his ribs, and one of them went through his right lung."

"It's serious then?"

He shrugs his shoulders, indifferent. We leave. We go through Valognes, it's market time. I think people look at me but I'm not sure about it. Their looking at me is like a grass snake sliding over a cold stone. They know me through Léon, who says of me, "Not snobbish," through Letellier, who finds me ugly, through my unsociability, which they mistake for a sign of bad health or haughtiness. Thus, our actions escape us, to be weighed by others who shape at will this strange aura called a reputation. As for me, I see them through a glass, they don't interest me, and I lose little by little my obsession about being displeasing to people.

We go toward Gettehou through the woods of Robey. The sea meets us at Saint Vaast. The wind blows, and we bathe in the iodine smell. The seagulls search the slime of the harbor at low tide, looking for a tired fish unable to get back into the open sea. The trawlers are loaded with hillocks of mussels, and the fishermen are shoveling them. I love this acrid smell, this salty wind, this bluish light.

I would love to be an animal.

We lunch on fish and roast veal, then we go to Tourlaville. It is early. The right-thinking people of the neighborhood come here to breathe a delicate fragrance of sulphur and utter an oh! of paternal indignation. Consider, a brother and his sister were in love with each other in this delightful manor under good King Henry. The lord of Ravalet, outraged, married his daughter to a wretched tax collector from Valognes, but the young girl escaped from her gaoler to rejoin her lover in Paris. Henry IV, like all former whores, had a kind of hypocritical menopause and ordered these children to be beheaded in the Place de Greve.

The last witnesses to their beautiful love are a fine old tower, a beautiful park of beech trees, and a glassy pool like a lifeless eye. Nothing survived from the execution of the two young offenders. Everything mourns them. Only, from time to time the green and golden frogs croak on the rotting rushes and disturb for a moment the stiff formation of the water lilies.

"I hope that you would have allowed me to be in love with my brother!"

"You have no morals, Céline; no more than I have, anyway."

"Fortunately, otherwise I would reject you. Why subject oneself to a strait jacket of hypocrisy placed on top of chopping blocks and stakes. My moral philosophy is harmony. If I feel a certain harmony between the world and me, I am moral. It is much more difficult to realize than it seemed to be at first."

We walk arm in arm under the high beech trees; I intertwine my fingers with Michel's and feel very close to him.

"Why did you show such indifference toward Auguste this morning?"

"Because he is just an old drunkard whose life is unimportant; he's had it. Prince could have killed you, Céline, and that's the only thing I was thinking about."

"And the pitchfork that I forgot."

"Yes; a peasant's daughter should not have made such a mistake."

The debate is closed. I don't dare to ask my father if he fears Julie and if so why.

"Do you know that I've been calling you Michel since my early years whenever I think of you?"

"Even when you were very young?"

"Don't make your voice so contemptuous when you speak of that child, she was your daughter!"

"I didn't despise you, Céline, but you were whimpering all the time, you were not pretty, and you were always hanging around my legs."

It's strange; I hear another voice saying to me: *Don't cry, make up your eyes, let me have some freedom. . . .*

"And *now* what do you think, Daddy?"

"I am amazed; you are intelligent, amusing, you resemble no one else, Célinette."

Someone else said that to me: *You are genuine, you resemble no one else.* I move closer to my father.

"Don't get tired of me, Daddy, love me always!"

"You are like a little girl at times, Céline."

How can I express my wishes to him: a growing tenderness, an exclusive tenderness; I would like to isolate ourselves from other people, in our favorite land. One cannot express tenderness well, this current, passing from one body to another to enliven inertia and affirm the freely chosen relationship. That dashing enthusiasm, is it not likely to break on a reef, Philippe? I do not wish to share Philippe, and Michel wishes even less to welcome him.

"I love you tenderly, Daddy. I don't want there to be any subject that is forbidden between us."

"This would be easier if you were my son!"

"On the contrary, your tenderness is more natural toward a woman."

"Yes, but this woman telephoned me one day to say that she was my daughter . . . and I had sufficiently forgotten it!"

"Consequently, on impulse, you first come to me because you love me, then you back up under the pretext that you are my father, then you come back reluctantly because, all things considered, you love me truly and I would even add that you would gladly suffocate me so that no one else but you had a share in me.

"Céline! You pick me like a crab! It's dangerous to be with an intelligent woman."

We choose to laugh, and nothing betrays complicity like shared laughter.

"You are exiling me to Mamie's tomorrow and Tuesday?"

"Yes, I prefer to. You wouldn't appreciate the company of the hired hands and you would be in the way."

He doesn't want me, either, to see him as a peasant cutting his hay. It's stupid. Why push me aside like a stranger? Perhaps it's because in their moments of harder work the peasants regain a kind of solemnity. I wouldn't belong there.

A bluish haze shades the horizon. The setting sun never inflames our skies, it just adds some long, dark-pink trails to the blue enhanced by the coming of the night. A popular saying is that this *rougie*, this reddening of the evening dries up the ponds and assures good weather. So Michel is satisfied.

"Let's go and see the sun go down from the top of Brick Cove."

This moor, perched high up, commands a view of the open sea. Outstretched in the heath, for a long time we watch the sun diving far away toward a line of haze: the phantom of La Hague. Everything is serenity. We are holding our breath. This hour is exceptional. Its calm penetrates me to obliterate the burning hatred. I chew a piece of grass and rub my back on the ground as animals do on the bark of the apple trees. Like them, I close my eyes with delight. Whatever happens, I'll be small, I'll be that nothing whose will power won't stop the sun from sinking in the evening behind La Hague. My long descent into Hell looks from here like drifting into intellectual masturbation. My land reminds me of a prime truth: simplicity. Michel holds my wrist, he presses his thumb against my pulse, and my life reassures his life.

The blue turns dark. The sea breeze rises with the tide; on the horizon the waves that lie down toward us are still, then they go back to the open sea. The boats will look like wrecks left on the dry sand. I yawn with pleasure. We return to a sleepy Hérouville.

Only Julie is awake. A hospital clerk has telephoned: Auguste is dead.

Papa says in a low voice that the funeral will take place on Wednesday morning, after the hay cutting. Julie mumbles that she has already made arrangements for the seven o'clock mass, the one for the destitute. I think of nothing. I go up to bed.

Something cold grips me. I am not going to be torn apart by Auguste's death. A death of no importance. And mine? I'll be entitled to a small paragraph in the Paris press. What would Philippe think? Philippe my bruise. How is it possible that each incident of my banal life brings me back forcibly to you? Once again this night will be a long night in which I will try to remember exactly that instant when your happy gaze became that of a man irritated by my presence, a hostile look . . . How could you not understand that the slightest animosity on your part hurled me toward the chasms of clumsiness where I became half-crazed, laughing too shrilly and saying absolutely anything. How stupid I must have looked! You who love beauty, laughter, graceful figures; you who love to be welcomed with open arms. You find suddenly in front of you a wretched and dejected hedgehog.

I remember those women who smiled at you. They used to whisper in your ear those words that caused smiles of self-satisfaction to flash forth from you. As for me, I watched incredulously, thinking that it was behavior typical of our social set; it seems so intelligent to appear to be always in love. If you had made love before my eyes I would have believed that you were fulfilling an eccentric bet! None is so blind as he who will not see. Somebody had the pleasure of opening my eyes. You quickly reproached my bitter words. The flow of spleen burning my mouth, ineffectively dammed up the litanies of love that I would have been able to tell you without tiring. Are you really human, Philippe?

Certainly I won't sleep tonight. I pull on my slacks over my pajamas, and I put a blanket over my shoulders. The night is sweet. A little thing comes rubbing against my legs whining. It is Grégole. In our dialect *gregola* means to shiver. Grégole is a tiny bitch, a mixture of all the bastard dogs in the neighborhood. She has survived in our yard for a few years, shivering with fear as soon as anyone touches her, feeding on meager scraps thrown out by Julie. The Normans don't like useless animals. I hold out my hand. Grégole jumps aside and starts trembling. I speak to her as to a child. She comes back. We go through the hedgerow of the garden. The last moon of June is full. I wrap myself in the blanket and lie down like a vagabond under the moon. Is there really under this bed of thick grass a stream that is the earth's blood? The ancients believed in such a *vouivre*, a generator of power for those initiated.

Grégole licks my face and comes to share my blanket. Why didn't I help this fragile being before this? This night is your night, Grégole. Auguste won't kick you any more, and I'm going to make you a queen.

The gray early hours awaken me. The dampness comes up from the soil and down from the sky. The earth drinks. It's the indecisive hour. The transparent moon fades behind the dull clouds, and the light of it adds a touch of light yellow to the horizon.

Perhaps the soul is made of white, never pure, of tarnished lights, and perhaps the black is merely a crescendo of blues? Have I perhaps mistaken the shadow for the light? Where does my disharmony come from? Know yourself! My *vouivre* is buried. I will find it again the day I stop backing away from myself. Never mind if I find it in violence.

I rise suddenly. Grégole runs away. I pull her back tenderly, for I don't want her to be hurt again by that solitude that makes her pupils dilate with fear. I look at this animal—ugly, yet beautiful in her wildness; clumsy, but passionate in the love that she is going to give me. Both of us are products of hasty copulations; nobody welcomed our arrival. She has kept from her life of abandon the wild eyes of the stray. I have kept from my solitary childhood the closed look of those who contemplate only themselves. I hold out my hands toward another me.

I fall on my knees so that Grégole is able to rub her nose against my cheek, and, distraught, she licks my eyes. You resemble a *fennec*, a fox of the sands, my dog, and I would not exchange you for the most beautiful female greyhound in the world. We are two lonely ones in this dewy field. But I am alone no longer, and neither are you.

I return to Hérouville, my blanket over my shoulders, my dog at my heels. On the doorstep I sense the storm.

"Céline, where were you? Where did you sleep?"

Michel seizes me roughly. Grégole runs away.

"I slept under the stars, against the hedge of the vegetable garden."

"I should have known! Ah, you are my daughter!"

He laughs. And his laugh is one of relief. What was he afraid of in his anxiety? Julie raises her eyes to heaven and pours our coffee in silence. All of her gestures having to do with my father are impatient ones. I had not noticed this before. Michel pays no more attention to her than he does to Grégole.

"I have adopted Grégole, Daddy; from today, she becomes a high-class dog."

"But she's a mongrel! Thursday I am going to Caen; I will bring you back a pedigreed dog."

"No, it's Grégole or nothing."

I prepare a dish for my dog. Up to now she has only known bread soup poured into a dirty bowl or bones thrown on the ground. When I give her a piece of meat, she moves away, quickly buries it, then hurriedly returns for another piece. She's saving them up for a rainy day.

Michel tells me to hurry up. Today they are cutting the hay, and I'm to leave for Vauville. I don't regret in the least, incidentally, this short exile. We cross Cherbourg in the early hours of the morning. The quays are jammed with the trucks of the fishermen. The mist hangs over the masts of the trawlers.

Something is bothering me, and I hide the fact poorly.

"Tell me, Daddy, I've seen Julie at the farm for as long as I can remember. How many years has she been with us?"

"I don't remember, your mother hired her."

"She has no family?"

"No she's a 'child of the hospital.' "

That's the way they used to describe the children looked after by the Public Assistance Organization. One used to go to "the hospital" to find a maid to perform slave labor.

"How old is she?"

"I've never thought about it. She was maybe older than your mother. I'd be happy if you could get rid of her, she's a pain in the arse."

I close my eyes. I cannot stand to see the one I love becoming vulgar. Michel's mouth is contemptuous. I think of the vulgarity of the feelings that Philippe hid behind polite words. He showed the same contempt.

"Julie has lived all her life at Hérouville, she tolerated Aunt Amélie without poisoning her . . . she had to tolerate you, too; we owe her something."

He is not pleased, but fortunately we arrive at Vauville. Grand-mère Mamie is completely taken by surprise when she sees me. She is an early riser. Her night ended hours ago, but she is still buried under ribbons, laces, and frills. She is happy at my arrival, but I upset her little world; she looks like a frightened mother hen who has lost her chicks. Bernard's mother cooks some eggs for me just in case I'm hungry. And I start a child's day; Mamie holds my hand, and we visit every corner in the house. I enter the holy of holies: her room. Under the lace bed curtains, cushions are piled high. My grandmother's bed is a mountain; I wonder how she can climb so high without getting vertigo. She shows me her principal pillow, then two round ones (her head props), one for each side of her neck, to support it. Sitting like this for hours, she waits for sleep as light as the foam of the waves. What does she think about as she contemplates the night? What is left of a life when the only thing to look forward to is death? I'm not listening to her endless prattle anymore. I look at the room, its generous proportions; the window overlooking the garden, then the narrow fields of La Hague outlined by low walls about the height of a sheep; the soil is not worth the price of the stones that enclose it! Within earshot is the sea, and the moors are only a stone's throw away. The garden wall is too high and restricts the view. Someone should trim the encroaching camellias; I will do it . . . I have already disregarded this fragile shadow who toddles, short of breath. Between death and me there is only that minute rampart of tired flesh; I feel cold with such a tête-à-tête. Reality and my heart will do battle, but I shall be biased.

We have a light lunch. Bernard comes to ask me shyly if I want to go for a swim. Why not? But my cure of youth is ended. Hopscotch is tiring once one has passed the age to play it. The wind catches us on top of the dune, it slaps us with such force that we become short of breath. We squat, taking shelter in a dale. The sand flies level with the ground, flattening the grass. Bernard closes his arms around me in a gesture of natural possession. I look at his face that shows no trace of having experienced any problems, the thick blond eyebrows upon which the wind has blown a few grains of sand. A face of which one tires quickly because one does not question what is hidden behind it. He wants to make love. He doesn't yet know the pleasure of inaction, the pleasure of the tired ones. I am all settled and sheltered from the wind and I need warmth. I change my tone quickly. Bernard has lost his shyness, but he has kept his spirit and roughness. I remember my first astonishment when Philippe taught me that two sexes had to have a delicate joust before being able to unite. I let his hands, full of gentleness, place my body under his, as one makes a child comfortable for sleep. He loved me too seldom, but it was enchantment when he did. One day I became invisible. He did not see my body any more. . . . I am wondering what I am doing there with this bore who is shaking me with his violent thrusts. I count the clouds, wrinkling my nose with discontent. I try to remember that "Venus has a thousand ways of making love" and that nothing is more healthy than love in the open air. Nothing doing. Ouf! It's finished! You won't catch me again.

He leaves me to go for a swim. He runs with long strides. How can such a beautiful ensemble of muscle and golden flesh shelter such emptiness? I begrudge him my brief moment of ecstasy. We could have played a whole season—but then I am accustomed to boredom; to loosen its ties would require a revolution. This child is nothing more than false hope ending in trivial action. Suddenly I laugh wildly. I think of Michel giving the slip to his ephemeral conquests and at the exasperated face of Philippe when one of his girls made a too lengthy farewell. Have I caught onto you, my two monsters, who occupy my life so completely?

"Céline!"

Bernard shakes himself and calls me. I make up my mind. The sun is warm but not enough to embrace the immense area of sand even less so the Channel. I have a superficial, icy wish.

"Come and have a swim, Céline."

"No."

"Don't sulk."

"I am bored."

He looks dismayed.

"But why?"

"Because you bore me."

His face drops like a child who has been denied dessert. The sadness of those one does not love is embarrassing. Nothing is easier to give than unhappiness!

I am weak. I don't have the courage to drop him there.

"You must excuse me, I am tired, I'm thinking of my next book, which makes me nervous."

Often at home one stops a newborn baby from whimpering with a pacifier. That's what I do now. My Apollo is silent and exhibits the grave face of somebody with a secret. And me, I have a fairly satisfactory escape.

We return without saying a word. Bernard's mother is waiting for us. She is worried: Mamie had a slight attack. I hurry to my grandmother's room. I see a timid little fieldmouse emerging from a bale of hay. Mamie, sheltered by her rampart of pillows, breathes in short gasps. She smiles weakly at me. I kiss her tiny hands, with their bluish fingers and prominent bones.

"It's nothing, my Céline, I am accustomed to these calls to order; give me my heart tablets."

From the night table I take a tablet from which I expect a

miracle. I move *The Imitation of Jesus Christ* and *The Thoughts* by Marcus Aurelius. Mamie has a complex spirit. Some pages are marked with a red taffeta ribbon. There, her thoughts are mirrored.

"Mamie, take care of yourself, Philippe is coming to see me Saturday. Mamie, he is coming . . ."

"I'll see him. I'll still be here on Saturday."

She says this resolutely. I want to believe her. I don't pray, but I suffer with everything in me that is capable of suffering. Suffering is the most beautiful prayer.

I sit near her in an easy chair. I watch over her as Grégole would watch over me. I would like my life force to reverse her decline; it would need so little. I listen passionately to her light breathing that does not disturb so much as a ruffle of lace. I try softly to raise a pillow or tidy the sheet. Philippe used to call me *chabraque* when I expressed my passion with strong gestures. One day I heard him call a woman *ma charmaresse*, his enchantress. I would have so much liked for him to call me that. He never did.

A small chime punctuates the night hours, those long hours when the flesh is miserable. I grow numb. I would like to drink. I remember my night of solitude. I drink. It seemed to me then that all misery grew quiet. From my body I felt only the beat of my blood pulsating through the arteries. I miss the being without substance, freed of everything to such an extent that when I had some brief moment of lucidity, I knew that it would have been possible for someone to take my life without my attempting any gesture of defense. The end of the drunkenness used to give me back my bitter combativeness.

Tonight, I have nostalgia for my annihilation, not to run

from myself but, on the contrary, to find myself, such as I would like to be: sweet, harmonious, relaxed.

In the morning Bernard's mother takes the next watch. I am going to bed.

My second day at Vauville is silent. Mamie regains some strength. I try to help her, powerless. She looks like an exhausted pilgrim gathering up her rags for the final leg of the trip. From time to time she winks at me, indicating "I'm holding my own." I explain to her softly that Philippe will come next Saturday, yes, in four days. I will invite him to Vauville.

"You will watch him, Mamie, you'll tell me what you think of him." (I don't dare to say: You who have almost second sight from beyond the grave, try to understand . . .)

But she understands perfectly well. Trembling, I leave her. Michel has come to get me at sunset. He is tired out. Those two days spent in the open sun have burnished his complexion and tanned his white temples. He examines the sky with a worried look. Will the hay dry before the next shower? There hasn't been either a storm or drizzle for eight days. Mamie's condition does not interest him.

"You can't have your cake and eat it, Céline. Your grandmother had her time."

He says this matter-of-factly. Michel is simple. He knows that a bee flying low indicates the autumn and that with the first white frost, winter is there. There can be a reprieve—but there won't be any pardon. Listening to him, I understand the fatalism of the peasants. I often labeled them narrowmindedly passive. I was wrong. They wisely avoid useless protests.

"Tomorrow morning, we bury Auguste."

"Have you arranged for the prayers?"

"Yes, some old people from Valognes."

The custom of going to pray is as old as our race. In each village we have accredited persons who, at each death, go from house to house to deliver the news and ask the people to come to the funeral. Such proceedings have the importance of a ritual. Julie sits, serves Calvados, and comments on each family associated with the mourning, starting with the family closest to the deceased. She makes sure that no one is missing. She religiously impales the macabre announcement on a long nail that already holds a complete cemetery, located between the post office almanac and the electric meter. Many lasting hatreds are born from omitting a name from the prayers' list.

Auguste is a pauper; his death is not an event locally.

With joy I find Grégole again. I try to convince her that one night in my room would be more comfortable than a night under the stars, but as soon as she comes into the house, she looks for a way out.

The next morning we leave early. Grégole watches our departure—Julie, black as an owl, Michel preoccupied with the hiring of a new hand. As for me, I am upset at the thought that the next funeral could be Mamie's.

Suddenly Grégole, who is sitting on her behind, starts a long lament, a gloomy song, her eyes closed, her nuzzle raised to the heavens. Hérouville is empty. Prince is chained to a stake, strong enough to hold a trawler. Grégole's howl resounds for a long time. No one will answer. It will be the funeral oration for Auguste.

It is only a short distance from the institution's chapel to the cemetery. Are we only ten, counting the priest and altar boy?

Léon, who is a freethinker, did not attend the mass. He follows the procession looking lost. Is he drunk? Auguste is buried in a pauper's grave. Then we go back home.

"Will you come to Caen with me tomorrow?"

An escapade with my father attracts me right away.

"Gladly, but in the evening we'll pass through Vauville to get the latest on Mamie."

That reservation annoys him, but he agrees.

We leave early on Monday morning. Michel goes to see his banker. He asks for a loan, which puts him in a bad mood. Alone, I discover Caen. When I visited there last, the tramps used to live in the ruins of the castle, and very often someone fished out a swollen body from the waters of the canal. I stroll. The city would now look like a model made by a talented architect if, around a street corner, one did not suddenly discover wonders from another age, the Abbey aux Hommes, either St. Peter or St. John, with a leaning look. I stumble over myself. A hairdresser's window reflects the insipid image of a youngish girl, with colorless hair, brownish eyes: a sad face for which one does not feel sorry.

A mad impulse grips me: a need to see my face no longer marked by failure. No, not seeing myself anymore, not recognizing myself anymore, becoming a new woman; and why not a golden sylph like the one who danced, reflected in the bottom of Julie's copper pots and pans? . . . I go in, I sit down, I speak firmly: I require very short hair; no, shorter; Venetian blonde, exactly like copper; also bleach the eyebrows and, since I'm changing everything, dye the eyelashes, too. Everybody busies themselves; the patience and kindness of provincial people surprise me once more. Little by little another Céline appears;

my face looks rounder, the red suits my complexion, my brown eyes seem less ordinary, my new eyelashes fringe my eyes. I wished to be completely unable to recognize myself, but I could not erase completely the stigma that had dulled my features.

I go to meet Michel. People look at me. Am I ridiculous?

"Oh, good God! Céline, you are a true Venus!"

Michel's surprise hurts me. Was I so ugly? He likes me like that; he pulls my hair, pats my cheeks. I take care of him; I choose for him a tweed suit, sweaters. He is happy, a beaming happiness. I feel responsible for his joy—and I am afraid of it.

We go through Vauville. After the exuberance of Whitsun, during which the whole of nature looks like the bouquet of a country bride, July announces maturity; the hay dries, the cattle are plump; the lamb has a flavor richer than at Easter; the milk has the flavor of the flowers eaten by the cattle since March, and the sky will wait until the end of next month to come down to us cloaked in fog. The frailty of Mamie seems like an anomaly.

She feels better and checks me out with an air of amusement.

"With your new hair style, you look like a Toulouse-Lautrec."

Laughing, I embrace her. I promise to come back to see her tomorrow afternoon. And I start my work. I don't want it. I swear to myself that it's not so, that all my actions are the usual ones, that my life beats normally. I'm not waiting for you, Philippe; no, I'm not waiting for you. Nevertheless, that Friday night I have not slept, and when at dawn Grégole sits under my window and starts whining to invite me to get up, I sigh contentedly; the night has at last ended. I panic because I don't know how to dress up. I reject a pair of slacks. I put on a very short kilt, white socks, and a white sweater. I make up my eyes and bristle my red feathers. I don't dare to look at myself. Julie clucks an "Oh!" and serves my coffee without saying a word. Michel is not there. I take his car. It is six o'clock. Valognes still sleeps. I like the morning peace of the provinces. (In the early morning, Paris is a city of open garbage cans.) The few people now awake must wonder where the Lemonnier girl is going at dawn. I don't know where I'm going . . . I meet the fishermen's trucks that are going down to Caen. At the station at Cherbourg, some families are waiting for their first summer visitors. People turn to look at me. Have I a strange look?

The train enters the station. What was the use of four years of hatred if I am moved just at the thought of seeing you again, Philippe?

His heavy build blocks the door of a car marked "Paris-Cherbourg." And everything disappears: the train, Cherbourg, the people, gray and anonymous, speaking loudly. I recognize his slightly heavy features, his eyes underlined with swollen rings, his hair cut short, his special kind of elegance made up of a harmonious ensemble in defiance of good taste. He carries on his left arm a folded raincoat and with his right arm swings the old black leather briefcase that I have seen him with for as long as I can remember.

Philippe, the platform of the station at Cherbourg belongs to you, you are at home everywhere, your natural gentleness makes you the liege-lord of the people and the scenery. Are you so tall that one sees only you in this early morning crowd? You, and your forty years of age, that have enjoyed too many nights of drinking, of discussing subjects that Socrates had dealt with so well before you. You are the type of man who doesn't know how to stay alone for a long time in his room. You live to the extent that you are able to communicate your ideas to others, but when the day comes that those people don't respond any more, they are no more to you than a dead tree. You are alive, Philippe.

Your eyes look for me. I guess what they are looking for! A worn pair of slacks, a tired pullover, dull hair—in brief, what is usually called a familiar shadow!

You wrinkle your forehead. You always wrinkle it like this when you're afraid of being bored, or of not easily convincing your interlocutor. Why would you fear me?

"Céline, what a nice surprise. You look great!"

I smile. I don't move. My coolness surprises him. Me, too. I was expecting to get a shock. I am only put out. I look at my husband like a thirty-year old woman who, judging her first experience, finds in it only a small dampened firework. I dreamed too often. My dream was an hallucination.

I take his arm. I press my finger on his forearm. How many times have I so pressed my fingers with the same possessive instinct?

"It's my property, and I'm holding on to it," as they say at home. But he was not my property, he was only the interest, and it took me a long time to understand it.

"How are you, Céline?"

"Better, thank you. Would you like us to have breakfast at the port?"

With pleasure.

A bluish haze halves the height of the city, and the first sun

84

of the day tints the houses of the Quay Caligny a garish pink. Cherbourg in the morning. My hyacinth town. I always went through your streets with a smile on my lips. A pink trail slides from the quay to the yacht basin and skims over the blue water. The mooring ropes whine. I love this world of the water.

We sit on the terrace of a café. The first auctioneer has closed his doors, but the entire port smells of the iodine of fresh fish. The gulls change direction, wings spread wide. They resemble wild geese; they have the same raucous cry, the same voracity. Their gray wings carry the white fuselages of their bodies toward the sun. And it is a wild ballet of air and water. I never tire of watching it.

"Your hair looks nice done that way. You could still have your hair shorter—you would gain in originality. You've put on weight."

There you are. Pygmalion has judged an object that doesn't displease him. He looks again at the port. I advance words like faltering pawns.

"Tell me about your journey to America."

"Oh, that was only a routine trip!"

But he tells me about it. It is an enchantment. Philippe is an excellent storyteller. He relieves me of the strain of making dialogue. Five years ago I got rid of my mediocrity in the hope that he would assume it in my place. How can I have given way to such easy thinking? Love is not a weir. One day he gave me back that gift that did not amuse him any more but suffocated him. I received it like a blow.

A voice over a loudspeaker startles me. It announces the time of the next tide. The swing-bridge pivots. One after the other, as slow as a Rogation Day procession, the trawlers leave the Bassin du Commerce heading for the open sea. The big bell of Trinity Church sounds the quarter hour.

"You remember the Laurentides? We went there from Montreal . . ."

I notice this "we," but it doesn't gall me. It's so far, the Laurentides. My own Laurentides—it is this yacht basin in Cherbourg where the seagulls dive like lance heads, their wings close to the body, and emerge dripping, live fish in their beaks. I follow the cruel game of the victor triumphing over the vanquished. *Vae victis!* Philippe speaks so naturally that I am wondering if I have not dreamed our disagreement. We don't look like a couple who are separated. In my despair I have often approached madness. Here, I have my soil under my feet and I don't like my cold heredity that forces me to see in Philippe's attitude a complete detachment toward me. Without noticing it, I hold out my hand to him to make him refuse it, thus confirming my disgrace. He takes it like any other hand.

I feel like laughing, I laugh at the absurdity of everything, at the comedy that we play, torn between the idea that we have of ourselves, what we really are and what we want others to think we are. I have never been Céline—I have been a cast-off of myself. I have been haunted about being what Philippe didn't like. As soon as he ceased to find me attractive, I became ugly; as soon as he stopped laughing, I became sinister; as soon as he treated me as a familiar object, I became persuaded of my uselessness.

Perhaps it was at the very second that I saw him again that my feelings, held down for so long, opened wide and projected him into "the world of others."

"Come, Philippe."

I got up. I see only the port, and the sea breeze skims the waters, blows up my kilt, and ruffles my hair.

"Come, I'll take you on the Smuggler's Walk to the round-house of the wreckers; come and see La Hague."

My invitation enchants him. He had expected to see a penitent face; he sees only a tall, gawky woman with newly reddened hair and a round face whom you first notice for her eyes, then, with a little attention, the tiredness of the features, pulling the mouth at its corners. He is intrigued. Who knows if my former gray presence was not for him the assurance of his powers over others?

I drive fast. The roads of La Hague wind tortuously around the farms and public wash house. I miss the crossing, and we find ourselves in the middle of a farm yard and hear a great flapping of white ducks. Philippe is delighted.

We are going to make a detour by way of the Bay of Ecalgrain, where one discovers the most savage of all beaches. I have never met anybody at Ecalgrain but the wind. We go down a sinking footpath. Suddenly, we are transported; the top of the beach is paved with small round pebbles worn by centuries of tides; each low tide rolls thousands of gray or pink pebbles to the open sea, and each wave, coming up, brings back the same pebbles to the foot of the cliff. No one could define this eternal rattling, mixed with the sharp clapping of the waters, that reverberate indefinitely in an echo that bounces against the cliffs. I close my eyes. Philippe is overcome. Those whom beauty touches are the chosen; they should dwell on the same bank and never torture each other.

In bravado, I take him to the dunes of Vauville. The wind

hurts his eyes. He walks carefully, avoiding holes. How fragile you are, my true love, in this setting created for rough men; nature pulls you off the pedestal on which I had placed you. You look like the tired seagulls, overburdened with their wings, who dream of shelter in which to sleep. In my frenzy of empty dreams I had not seen you like that: a man marked by time.

"What do you think of this view?"

"It is grandiose, overwhelming even."

"It doesn't overwhelm me. It's my chamber of love. I come to frolic here with a handsome twenty-year old teacher."

I'm barely aware of being ridiculous. I brandish my first act of independence like a trophy.

"He must be lacking in technique."

"He starts a new fire from the ashes of his old one!" I banter. No man can stand someone praising the amorous exploits of another man without feeling at the same time emasculated.

"Have you the whims of an old lady? And do you try to gratify them without risking your liking for domination?"

"When you take an eighteen-year-old virgin, do you call that the whim of an old man?"

"Yes, that is the whim of an old man."

There, I'm hoist by my own petard. Philippe's worst fault: he is honest with himself. I am crestfallen.

"To tell you the truth, he bores me. I could try to occupy my brain by trying to remember the verses of *The Eighty Hunters*, but I have never been able to remember them."

He bursts out laughing.

"I like your kind of humor, Céline!"

"You have often scolded me for having an unsophisticated sense of humor; it is true that I've never been very adept at dry

88

humor and making use of other people's clever witticisms. At home, we season the soup with coarse salt and call an arse, an arse!"

"I have never complained about that; you are mistaken."

For the first time since his arrival, we dare to look at each other face to face. We are on the verge of a dialogue. Would he settle our quarrel? Would we settle accounts? Philippe guesses my thoughts.

"All this is unimportant. What would be the point in sharing the mistakes evenly? Our common life is no more than a distant and unsuccessful experience."

"I am not even sure of having loved you."

"Why are you denying yourself, Philippe? Your love was not cowardice, and it's not true that because a person has ceased to live that he has not lived. One can never judge a love outside its context; it is as if you were to extract a snail from his shell. Our dead enthusiasms always humiliate us. Who knows, however, if in those moments we are not truly ourselves?

"Let's say, that I was captivated by the pure and melancholy girl that you were. Your innocence became a sort of intransigent unsociability, and your melancholy turned to bitterness."

"I must have had bad company!"

We walk with short steps along a path so narrow that we are elbow to elbow, both trying to find ourselves. We don't look at each other.

But why has he come? I get scared. I feel a contest has begun without me. I have been considered a quantity not to be taken into account. My taciturn ancestors, bargaining for their cattle, taught me to be suspicious. My instinct is aroused.

"Come, Mamie is waiting for us to have lunch. You are the big event of the year for her."

"I didn't know you had a grandmother."

"Nor I. I saw her sometimes when I was a child, but my father didn't care for her. That was sufficient excuse for her to be indifferent to me."

We enter the village. Philippe, I know exactly what you are thinking at this moment: You look amused at this small village from another world, squeezed against hills covered with ferns, divided by a brook that the peasants cross by walking on gray granite blocks as wide as tombstones, and beyond the dunes sings the surf of the sea. You say to yourself: How pleasing it must be to write here. Yes, here genius blossoms like gorse at Easter. But one must know how to listen to the wind; one must be able to face the open sea without sinking into a whirlpool of anxiety. One must be able to stay alone with oneself. And you don't realize it, but here you would have no audience.

Mamie is waiting for us. She is wearing a lovely gray silk dress that makes her look like a marchioness, and she has dressed up her hair with a veil dotted with velvet flowers. She is full of curiosity. Philippe is quite taken with her, and he becomes a man who, in being nice, is delighted with himself for being so. Mamie has invited her attorney and the mayor of Vauville. So I start my act. I whine about my bad health, which doesn't seem to improve. Now's my chance, I'm feeling my way. Philippe thinks that I'm putting on an act of respectability brought about by the presence of my grandmother's guests. He goes one better by saying that the air agrees with me. I embroider further: All Saints' Day is still far off, but I need a few more months to get on my feet again. Mamie gets the idea that Philippe intends to take me with him to Paris. She begs him with tears in her eyes to let her granddaughter stay. Philippe swears to her that I may stay in Vauville as long as I want to.

Oh, Mamie, love, forgive us, we splash you with our mud. Since you have had the cleverness to invite the most prominent people of the district, I take advantage of it and I make my husband say in front of reliable witnesses that I agree completely with what he says: I must take care of myself. That I have not completely abandoned the marriage bed could now be proved by the most ineffective witness.

If Michel were there, he wouldn't fail to notice the calculating tone of my voice.

The mayor of Vauville is an ocean fisherman, a simple man, tall and thin like the ancient men of La Hague, with skin reddened and hardened by the sea air. He doesn't grasp this tale of poor health; the only time his wife even took a rest was when the priest came to say prayers for her dying. I am sure that he despises me. And he's right. Besides, I always gave credit to those who were despising me.

Mamie's attorney is a rotund man with red hair. He came to start practicing in Beaumont to make money; the practice he took over didn't cost him very much, but La Hague is the poorest place in the whole Cotentin region. He champs at the bit, dreaming of the distant day when he will be able to practice in Coutances, or even Caen.

What are we doing there, sitting around this table, the only thing we have in common? Our preoccupations take our minds far away from our bodies. Nevertheless, after the coffee Mamie is going to ask her attorney if "everything is ready." He will smile as usual, but not Mamie. She gets ready for her journey, and I can sense that the thought of that beyond so close consumes her. She looks at Philippe with a surprised look in her eyes. She rather likes him. I guess that she may tell me: "Your husband is a seagull, you should have been his rock." The trouble is that a rock doesn't ask to be happy. I do.

Our guests leave. Philippe has charmed my grandmother; he made her laugh and I was almost shocked. Mamie goes upstairs to take a rest and let us discuss our "projects." I settle back into a big deep armchair. Philippe would like to leave now but his train does not depart until five P.M.; we are condemned to two hours of confrontation.

I don't just look at him any more—I watch him. Philippe, in all your life you have never seen a bloody duck that has just had its head cut off, flying. Weakness also has its moments of rejuvenation. A cold anger fills me. I am not good any more at putting up with everything. I keep quiet and bow my head. I am a wall.

"Céline, when do you expect to go back to Paris?"

"Not before the end of the summer."

"Do you want to keep the apartment?"

"For whom?"

"For yourself, of course!"

"I haven't thought about it. I'll see later on."

"I need to know. Listen Céline, it's time to straighten out a situation that no longer means anything. I need a divorce, now. Be decent enough to make things easy for me. I met a young English girl in New York, and she is exactly the kind of woman I have always been waiting for."

I don't listen to what follows. I look at his face. Since his arrival, he has been in turn restrained, irritated, stubborn, at least polite. Suddenly he relaxes; his features become youthful. Philippe has the blissful look of those who live in the state of grace that is happiness. He is in love and could speak of this woman for hours; she is still a source of wonder.

He doesn't remember for a single moment what we once were for each other. I no longer exist. Like the young viper that winds itself around the stem of a foxglove and points a tiny hissing triangular head, I make a forward motion with my head. I despise you, Philippe. Perhaps because, in spite of you, I was holding on to a foolish hope that your joy now wipes out.

I know that I am going to say no. No, to make him suffer, to make her wait, to make sure that what I cried for was not in vain. I close my eyes. I cannot stand his happy face any more.

"You want things to drag as little as possible so that your maiden doesn't see you getting old."

"Don't be mean. You will get old, too, and in a sadder way than I."

"That's not certain. Right now I want to have a peaceful summer, I will think about our marital problems after All Saints' Day. They have been on my brain for four years, and I feel nauseated. Me, *I'm* in no hurry."

"You! *You!* You are an egotistical monster; you retired within yourself many years ago, passionately fond of your misfortune; hanging on to illusions, you live in a hole. Why do you hate me? I did not swear to you eternal fidelity. The day I ceased loving you, I told you. I have always been frank with you."

"That's true, Philippe; you even introduced me to all your mistresses."

"And how many did you think I had?"

"Philippe—tell me that at least once you were moved by my sorrow."

"Never! I got the impression that the gods had brought Cassandra back to life, setting her at my heels. What a sinister spectacle that woman built as a permanent reproach! One feels guilty of everything, even of living—even of laughing. Well, as for me, I like women who make me laugh."

"You start to get me really angry! I have known you to be beaten, drunk because you were full of fear, ridiculed by your conquests. The woman you are searching for, you'll never find —you want her to be perfect and you wouldn't be able to stand her perfection because she would make you look mediocre. This one, you will destroy as you did me because you will dread that day when you will understand that she has only the animal desire to be loved and to be protected by this love. All of us love the same way. And you abhor feeling responsible."

"Your hatred blinds you; no dialogue is possible with you."

"What you call dialogue is only a long monologue to your glory."

"You are stupid, my poor friend; your book, let me remind you, came into being through *my* glory. At least be grateful."

"The next one will be *my* book. The book of a woman adult and free at last."

"Well, you can have it read by your teacher after dinner; he will correct your mistakes in French. By the way, does he spit out his chewing gum before making love?"

"And you, do your prostitutes douche before they spread their thighs?"

"You sink quickly into that filthy vulgarity which is your true nature."

"No, into an earthy realism for which I don't need a smile or a clever face."

"I refuse to take part in this kind of conversation. I loathe peasants: They are boorish, stubborn, and narrow-minded. You are as pig-headed as a *chouan*.* Take me back to Cherbourg."

My throat and eyes are burning so that I choose the route by instinct. Philippe, for so long I avoided words and complaints, how have I been able to scream like this? How have we come to this point? We have lived together. This book that you now ridicule, it was you who made it come to life. When we traveled—how many times as you listened to me painting a bold portrait of the women who passed within reach of my teeth did my realism charm you till you were crying with laughter? How many times, waking up, did I surprise you looking at me sleeping? Why this vacuum, then, this mud, this hatred? For a woman? One more . . . an Englishwoman? another one?

We have no more duties to each other, Philippe. And, yet, I know that a fruit falls because it is ripe—or because a storm knocks it down.

"My decision is taken. Your delaying tactics won't change anything. Good-by, Céline."

He is gone.

I walk around like a robot, but I know that my footsteps will take me to the sea. I need to know that beauty exists; I am

*A Norman royalist in the French Revolution, a guerilla fighter.

going to hold out my hands toward it, and I will find it, serene, simple, lasting. I grip the parapet of the swing-bridge. I get the wind in my face; it buffets me, ruffles my skirt, intoxicates me, caresses me. I still say no. My refusal is unimportant. My revolt is like a jellyfish stranded on the beach at low tide. I do not suffer; I am like the convalescents in a hospital whose sickness comes up from the depths of their being, fading their skin. And this evening I think that love can be a punishment.

Michel has been waiting for me. We don't talk about Philippe. But his silence is not a sign of indifference. He guesses that after having respected the truce imposed by normally good standards of behavior, our dialogue has been that of any couple that has separated. We have skinned each other. We have taken part in a match where all blows are allowed, particularly low ones. By now Philippe is white with rage, shocked by my vulgarity. And as for me, I feel like being sick.

Why have we released two phantoms in this way: mine, that of a humiliated woman; his, that of a woman imprisoned in her egoism? Why am I the only one accused? It's true, Philippe. Losing your love, I hastily built a shelter of semiconfinement; deprived of your refuge, I tried to find in sickness a sheltered world. It is easy to be a sick person; you just have to drink and not sleep, practice your anguish; you build a special kind of personality, and others hesitate to cross your path. The universe of women is small—it quickly becomes a jail.

Michel settles down in front of the television set. I sit at his feet and rest my head against his thighs. The mad temptation to live a closed life at Hérouville is strong. Just the two of us, bound up together. I am not sure, at the moment, that Michel does not envisage such a way of life. He is fascinated, but he hesitates. Why? Would this look like madness? Would it be unnatural? Would it be successful? I'm not sure that it would be easy.

Upstairs we go to bed reluctantly because sleep separates us. The same secret plan saddens us. We look like children who roll shiny, sweet-smelling blackberries. Suddenly, they squash the fruit, and there is only pulp left, the purple juice staining the skin.

I have known only one kind of happy sleep: near Philippe. Since then, each time that I touch a bed I feel that I'm lying down to die. My sleep is a drudgery or compulsory service that I owe to my body. Finally I swallow a sleeping pill.

July is no more. The first August evenings are mild; under other skies one would think it a pleasant springtime. It is the time of the long twilight. I live close to Michel and Grégole. I do some writing. Michel moves away, annoyed by an occupation that to him seems useless. Grégole cannot stand the uneven tapping of my touch. As for me, I regain the assiduity I had as a student to approach the mystery that is a woman's thought. I feel flowing through me a serenity against which the habit of unhappiness can do nothing. Suffering, they say, is honey that every writer stores on his shelves. It is manna. I take out my honey flavored with the bitterness made of the wild essence of my childhood; or honey with the acrid taste of ashes from my hours of misery, a bit of honey sucked from the blooming hawthorn and the pink hoods of the Whitsun apple trees. It is a strange mixture. But not for one moment do I have the temptation to write anything untrue. I squeeze out the words from deep down inside me, and often they bring tears to my eyes when they burst out.

I write with force; suddenly I have a lot to say. Philippe is no longer here, and I cannot rush to him at the end of every page to ask his advice. He has cut my umbilical cord; but no matter, I survive without his approval. Freed from my morbid confinement, I descend carefully, first with curiosity, then passionately, within myself; I use the scalpel to peel my life of its outer covering. I will reach that naked soul that I dreaded the existence of only by passing through a distorting prism.

My favorite recreation is to watch the flight of the wild duck. We go on the marsh at sundown. Michel takes cover. The tall, broad silhouette of my father becomes my only horizon. I contemplate him there, relishing his power to give death, spattered by the evening light that falls into the march and sparkles on the surface of the water before sinking in it. He is overwhelmed by the savage beauty of the scenery and by the devout admiration that I dedicate to him. He is happy. Mamie is happy, too, when I am near her. Have I ceased to be the one whose presence kills all joy? All that was necessary was to be me—a happy me.

One evening, Grégole brings to me in her jaws a sauvagine, the wild waterfowl sticky with blood, a body so warm that the blood steams with life. I take it in my hands, and its blood floods me, covers me like a wave: I am a bleeding bird, hurt in the neck with an open wound, I bow a limp head to my breast and I split open, my entrails heaving, as if everything that was inside me had to run out of my gaping mouth. Michel drops his gun to grab hold of me, collapsed, shaken by endless nausea. Long after sundown I am still lying with my head against my father's leg. The plants of the marsh give way to make me a bed.

I think of the dunes of Vauville, of the boy who, in the enthusiasm of youth, mounted me with a great ardor, as Prince performs in the glory of his finest hours. And the same abundance! Everything is beautiful; I am aware of my body—it is boundless.

The next time I see Bernard I will look at his eyes and his nose, too. I think that he has a handsome nose. But I may be wrong!

We go back very slowly. Michel curses. Letellier's dog comes out of Hérouville, and Grégole howls. Michel denigrates the Lord rudely.

"That slut Grégole is in heat!"

"She's not a slut because she's in heat, Daddy. Don't be silly; she's normal, that's all!"

"I don't give much for her skin if Letellier surprises her playing around in his yard."

"I don't give much for his skin if he kills my bitch."

My Grégole finds herself tied up with a rusty chain. She looks at me, a begging look in her eyes. Eventually, probably, Papa will kill the Letellier's dog.

The next day, I train her on the leash, both of us toddling along with short steps. The apples are ripe, and the cows bang their heads against the young trees. The green fruit falls, and the cattle regale themselves with the tart flesh.

We pass a plump Norman woman, short stemmed and pink as a May sky, except that, in fact, the skies of May are sometimes blotched. She stops.

"Céline!"

I look without recognizing her, a clean-smelling woman who is wearing a girdle too tight for her, who has her hair drawn back behind her neck; she has a shy look, her eyes marked by sadness.

"Céline, I am a cousin of your mother's!"

I leave my dead to their earth and can only think: here's the girl friend of Daddy! My eyes become cynical, I stare at this stranger with arrogance, I am tempted to tell her: "So you're the obliging lady who is waiting for Sunday?" So Daddy lays his big body on top of this fat flesh? But he must have the feeling he's cuddling a featherless goose!

"I've been waiting to meet you for a long time. I asked your father. Did he tell you?"

"No."

I have fired my arrow. It was a bull's eye. I see her blink.

"Shall we walk a little, since chance has brought us together?"

"If you want to."

"My name is Marie."

I do not dare to say: I couldn't care less; so I say: "Ah!" I barely hide my aggressiveness.

Marie suffers but she holds on. She is aware of my hostility. She frowns and chooses her words. I know that the beginning is the most difficult part; everything that she has on her chest will follow like a torrent breaking a dam. So I don't help her.

"Do you like it at Hérouville?"

"Yes, it's my house. It's a little lacking in comfort, but I'll attend to that."

"You . . . you intend to stay here?"

She turns her face toward me. How anguish changes her face! The pink turns to gray, everything that is round becoming flabby. Marie blinks.

"Listen to me, Céline. I have known your father for twenty-five years. He's a man of fire. He has discovered you, you are new, and he lets himself be consumed, you think; but he will consume you, too; Michel always takes more than he gives. I know it only too well! What will become of you at Hérouville? Here, after the September equinox, the rain starts to fall, and it will not stop before Easter. You are a writer, but you will not write for ten hours every day. What will you do in that ramshackle house, icy with dampness, more cloistered than a nun?"

"I will have central heating put in."

"That won't stop the rain from overflowing the gutters and the night from falling at five o'clock! Your people did wrong by you, but they are still your people. They taught you a certain way of living which is not ours. Your return to your roots diverts you, but it will weigh heavily on you. How will you react to your father then? Who can say if he won't get tired of you. I have seen him getting tired so often!"

Marie's voice breaks. I have the immediate enjoyment of any woman who sees another one suffering. She, too! That must be it: the relief of shared ridicule or, better still, the hope that one has at last found someone more pitiful than oneself.

"You have known . . ."

"Oh yes! Someone wrote to me. Here there are still poison pens; someone told me, and I have often seen it for myself."

"Why did you put up with it?"

"I loved him. You accept the man you love. Or you don't love him. You must love with lucidity; you try then to lose as little as possible. As for me, I have accepted everything as if nothing mattered, as if, in your father's life, I was the only constant element; I have minimized everything else. He has finally come to look at things in the same way."

"But that's awful, Marie. Michel has used you and has sacrificed you."

"I have not lost the man I loved."

Marie, the stubborn. You tell me calmly about a love that you have protected from hatred, a love that you have steered like a lifeboat, taking the waves and bailing constantly. You kept watching the lighthouse. Marie with the round cheeks and the blotched face, we taught you to play the piano. And you got an educational diploma; you know how to embroider initials on a sheet, and you apply in your daily life that which a woman far more cultured than you—whom you have never read—has written: "To love with your eyes open is perhaps to love distractedly like someone insane; it is to accept all madly."

And without trying, you beat me. Even though I don't want to give you the palm so easily.

"And Julie, have you accepted her? She hates you."

"My cousin, your mother, never loved your father, he had too much of a sexual drive for her taste, she was forever running away from him. It may seem impossible to you, but Julie was not ugly. She was the one there when he had nothing to satisfy his appetite. She stayed. She represents the darker side of Michel's nature; he gave her the worst thing he had: his instinct. He's been wanting to get rid of her for a long time. She is no more than a creature of hatred and habit, but she serves him well, and it would look bad if he freed her. As for me, I knew that as long as she remained at Hérouville, no other woman would get her foot in except you."

She almost begs me to pitch my tent somewhere else. I am tired, and that is enough for today. This woman tells me simply that I have inherited Michel's monstrous egoism. Like him, I am demanding and return little; if I give, I choke. We are a strange lot. But we are from the same race. This reassures me.

"Don't tell Michel that we met. One of these mornings I'll come and see you when I'm walking Grégole."

"I'll be waiting for you."

I go, feeling tired. My stomach feels as if it were being squeezed. Must I call Dr. Carpentier? What am I to think about Marie? I let myself fall on the grass. I stay there, prostrate around an imaginary or real cocoon. I will go to see Marie sometime soon. I don't like Hérouville anymore. Julie is too depressing. I prefer Vauville. Now I bring up a wave of bitterness that burns my throat. I touch my stomach and burst into a happy laughter that curls my lips. Grégole rushes forward and licks my eyes.

Philippe, a son is promised to you! He will not have what I liked so much in you: that straight mop of hair, so silky that I was losing my fingers in it in my adoration when you first slept on my breast; in the morning you looked like a feather duster, and I called you Byron. If only nature could perform a miracle!

There are two full weeks before Whitsun. I will try to vomit discreetly. But how will I tell Philippe . . . I am delighted. Not even distressed. Really, I am reserving a surprise for him, and it's a big one! I laugh to myself because he'll think that Bernard didn't spit out his chewing gum. I feel strong. I flower. People tear me apart physically and spiritually, and I say: so much the better. I deny everything.

I am young. Hatred consumed me, but it did not dry me up. I pull out the green grass in handfuls without the gesture having any importance. The earth will produce other grass. And I, too, am going to produce. . . .

Michel comes through the gate as I arrive.

"Come with me, Célinette. I'm going to make a quick call at Crasvillerie Manor."

I stuff Grégole into the car, and the three of us leave. The air is mild, almost hot.

"We're going to go through Gonneville. Your grandmother Phellie was a native of that place. She's buried there, and my sister Amelie. The deputy mayor told me that the grave had been damaged by the winter rains. I must have it recemented before next autumn. We'll probably see Adrien, the Gonneville gravedigger. I might as well warn you, whatever you do, don't laugh when he says to me very seriously that if, by accident, I happen to die before he does, he will dig me a well-shaped grave, and it will be a tip-top job . . .

"What?"

"Yes, I untangled his old-age pension for him; since then, he promised me with gratitude a very beautiful grave. The simple people have little to give, but their work. Let's go and see Adrien."

Gonneville is a tiny village buried in the valley of a little stream, its castle decaying inside the square of its stagnant moat. The cemetery is nestled against the church. Adrien is there. He is bent toward the earth that he has dug so many times. The spadefuls thrown by the thousand over his shoulder have developed the muscles of his arm, but the rest of his body seems to be wasting away. He stops ripping open the soil and crosses his arms, resting on a spade as tall as he. His face is bright red and his teeth rotten.

"It's hot, Adrien."

He nods his head, scrutinizes me carefully, and asks a question in dialect.

"I don't mind if I do," Michel replies. Adrien bends toward the empty open grave and draws on a rope, holding the knots in the palm of his hands very carefully. The neck of a bottle emerges. Instead of a corpse, the hole is cooling a bottle of cider. Adrien offers us a drink. He winks his eye in my direction, asserting that his cider is "strong." My poor friend, when Philippe taught me to drink vodka I found it strong, and it was more powerful than your apple juice, even if the latter may contain a few drops of sulphuric acid! I down it. Adrien clicks his tongue. He confides to Michel that he finds me "not stuck-up," which is, in our part of the country, the greatest of compliments.

This field of the dead is peaceful under the noon sun. The deaths of others do not bother me greatly. I rest against a granite cross. We drink a second glass. Adrien must think that enough is enough, for he corks the bottle, puts the slip knot of his rope around its neck, and the bottle starts again its slow descent into the entrails of the earth. He dries his mouth with the back of his hand and contemplates my father.

"It's not to bring you bad luck, Mr. Lemonnier, but if by chance . . ."

Looking at the horizon, I wrinkle my forehead. Michel thanks Adrien as he has done so many times when promised a carefully dug grave.

We walk to Grand-mère Phellie's grave, the goal of our trip.

Yes, both grandmother and Aunt Amelie are "taking water." Michel shrugs a fatalistic shoulder, which means: in any case, they won't die by drowning! My father doesn't worship the dead, he has far too good health for that.

Adrien salutes us and warns us that the steps of the cemetery are "a bit worn." He warned us too late. Michel is already sitting on his broad behind. And we burst into laughter. I pick up my father, and we go to La Crasvillerie.

"How much cider does Adrien drink in a year?"

"Oh, like all the old folks of these parts, he drinks his harvest in winter and, to wait for the next, he drinks two or three barrels bought from a neighbor better stocked than he."

"That must fill the municipal laundry pool to overflowing!"

"It sounds like a problem for a primary-school diploma! Let's suppose that you have a dry laundry pool: you fill it with three barrels and the harvest of ten apple trees, what is the capacity of the wash house and what is the capacity of the stomach of the Norman gravedigger?"

"Let's suppose that the Lemonnier girl happens to go by and she has a throat as dry as July thatch and as stiff as the point of Hoc—"

"Let's suppose that a parish counselor weighing ninety kilos falls into the laundry pool and makes it overflow—"

To my great enjoyment, we go on supposing endlessly. I had gone searching for my lost youth, and I have found it with delight. I would like to keep playing with my father as children do until the game tires them out and they fall asleep.

But, through a hedge of tamarisk twisted by the west wind, we can see the somber granite turrets of La Crasvillerie.

The farmers of Val de Saire have chosen one of the most

beautiful Norman manors in which to set up their artificial insemination cooperative. In the past, we received our sexual education in the farmyards where, in open air, people "bring the cow to bull." It was a violent sight, which often lasted as long as an hour, on the dry hay or in the hay loft. Now, you get marked sperm samples rated as being from either good or very good donors. Times have changed.

I think about Bernard: What a fine animal!

I haven't the stomach to go and see a bull perform. I have never been a voyeur. I wait for Michel in the car. He doesn't come back. He is one of those people for whom time has no value. Such people are on their way to extinction. When he comes back, I have been waiting for him so long that I would gladly throw Grégole in his face.

When you get right down to it, this man is a boor. I was wrong to try to make a god of him. How wrong it is to try to deify humans.

"I'm going to take you for a visit."

"I don't want to go."

"Listen, stubborn. Do you know where?"

"I don't give a damn."

He bursts into bellowing laughter that makes Grégole tremble. As for me, I look at his swelling throat, his head thrown back to allow him to laugh more freely. I forgive everything.

"We are going to say hello to the Marquis and the Marquise of Grèves."

"Oh yes!"

I am fifteen again . . . and Michel keeps laughing.

Neville is the most desolate beach that one could wish for, a pebble beach that plunges into the sea. The slope, the tides, the rocks at the water's edge would have been enough to discourage any invader. People ask why the Germans built their impregnable blockhouses here if not to shelter the seagulls—and the Marquis de Grèves and his Marquise.

In this tormented setting, facing the open sea, for about twenty-five years, these two ghosts have lived in a citadel of concrete. Hung on rusty iron rods some rags fly in the wind. At low tide the Marquis fixes a fishing net between two strong poles. I see a frail black silhouette standing against the entrance to the building. She contemplates the open sea. She is the red-and-black shadow of a worn-out woman. Who could tell without knowing the sex of those bones dressed up in black?

In a low voice Papa confides to me that the inside of the blockhouse is jammed with empty bottles. At the last autumn equinox, the sea engulfed the place and for a long time the waves have been breaking the glass on the cement walls. The peasants pick up the fragments in the surrounding fields, fearing the worst for the feet of their sheep. Michel supposes that a new equinox would be needed to clean up the place and empty the corpses and garbage of a full year.

He salutes and asks if everything goes well. The Marquise slowly turns her puffy face toward us.

"Bad luck, Monsieur Lemonnier, bad luck!"

"And what bad luck?"

"I no longer remember when, but at some time people gave my poor man a pair of boots; people are dirty, sir! Those boots have rotted his feet."

I see Michel stifle a gasp. We find the truth soon enough. At the Cherbourg hospital they cleaned the Marquis like a pig with detergent and a hose. But he had not removed his shoes for so long that a nail had stuck into the sole of his foot and the flesh had rotted. In taking off the boot the nurse took off the foot as well!

Everyone makes his own truth. We all fabricate our own paradise. The Marquise has a dapper companion who is contaminated by an unhealthy benefactor. What a society!

She has spoken enough for today. She goes back to her dream at the point where we interrupted it. We don't exist any more.

Daddy drops me at Vauville. Mamie lavishes her delicate affection on me. Mamie—the people of Vauville always judge her with respect: "a little eccentric" because during her whole lifetime she has loved feeling the raindrops on her face, the spindrift, beauty, out-of-the-ordinary people. With the greatest of modesty she knew how to hate vulgarity. Refined but passionate, she had soon learned the melancholic resignation of the sailors' wives. Is it from her that I have taken my special aptitude to suffer? She lived at Hérouville and I can imagine her reading her favorite authors while letting my mother grow up like a skinny cat. She abandoned that unworked farm as quickly as possible to her son-in-law whom she would have been unable to stand. As for me, she loves me. Just so. There was a miracle that has made of me a thing of hers, and of her a thing of mine. Nobody can replace the one in the eyes of the other. She is my own, and the approach of death makes her even more dear. I often think that All Saints' Day is far away. Has she still sixty days of life left before her?

Bernard runs away from me. I catch up to him with a sudden tenderness. I stroke the curve of his nose, I smooth his eyebrows. He misinterprets my feelings. I push him away with my index finger smiling. He turns his back on me. Let's hope that my son has neither my beauty nor the intelligence of this clodhopper. My God, I pray to you, above all, don't make any mistakes in your distributions of resemblance! It would be a disaster!

He comes back, exhibiting his sadness like a reproach. But I don't feel guilty; what have I done, except to bite into a beautiful orange and throw away the peel? Next month, the first day of school will call my lover to the local school at Laigle. He will give to the little Normans courses of instruction in civics. And I won't see him again.

I have no news from Philippe. He must be spending a serene vacation, which is a forerunner of autumn, in the corner by the fire of high society in Paris. A great love, shared by a great public, what can you ask for that's more touching than that?

It has been raining for the past few days. A never-ending rain that runs off my roof in singing cascades. I write. Michel selects the cattle that he will sell at La Sainte-Croix-De-Lessay fair on the twelfth of September. I will not accompany him. I don't like to hear him speaking in the local dialect, and I cannot stand to have the places that Barbey used to love losing their mystery and suddenly stinking of fried potatoes. When I was a child, for the feast of the Holy Cross the women still used to wear the coif of fluffy lace like blossoming hawthorn hedges, and the wind of the dunes of St. Germain-Sur-Hay used to stir their ribbons and shawls. All that is dead. Marie is right. That world is no longer mine. But it has left a tie of granite deep inside me. Who can know that I wear it?

This evening, it is still raining endlessly; the house looks like the Ark under the rain. What will become of it two months from now when the only trace of life will be the green grass of the close and the whole of nature will have taken on her dull tones of putrefaction?

Night falls, and the barn owl starts to hoot. I bang the shutters of my window to scare it. It keeps quiet a short while, then, announcing the night, starts its song again. Hérouville resmbles a jellyfish. Nobody reacts. The only light in the house is in Julie's kitchen. Julie frightens me now. I bang my shutters again—I would do anything to silence this bird. I call Michel.

"Fire a shot at it, Daddy, I can't stand that hooting!"

"You're crazy! What did it do to you, that bird? If you had heard the hissing of a viper I could understand it, but for a poor barn owl who sings because it's the hour when she must sing . . . there is no need to make such a commotion. In five minutes she will have finished. If I fired a gun, Letellier would immediately call the gendarmes at Valognes and tell them that strange things are happening in my place!"

He shrugs his shoulders. The barn owl has stopped her singing. I open my fingers. I have such misgivings of bad luck that I would like to curl up against Michel to reassure myself in his warmth. It is time to confront my fears. Or not to have them anymore. I dress the table without a word. We have dinner early and watch television, our schedule, as regular as the barn owl's singing. I am bored. Upstairs, I open my icy sheets. I remember long ago Aunt Amelie with a long-handled copper warming pan filled with scorching-hot coals that warmed for a short time the damp cold of the bed. Entangled in a nightdress that had belonged to my mother, I was searching eagerly for that patch of warmth that seemed to me like tenderness. . . .

Tonight, I am alone. As lonely as the child who slept there a few years ago. The water streams from the roof, and the first strong gusts of wind that forecast an early autumn shake the hedgerows. Why does the autumn come so early this year? Léon will say once more that the seasons are not what they used to be. Why doesn't Philippe write to me? Surely they must need *my* point of view concerning the divorce proceedings! How far along is he with his project? Has he been disappointed by his infant? She is probably what I used to be: an outline of a woman. As with me, he will attempt to recreate her to his taste. Although I was willing, did I stop too soon being a shadow to dare to claim back my true self? Philippe, you can't escape that rule that sees man as the builder of the ideal woman. Your imagination is such that your desire grows out of all proportion. You justify your failure by thinking that it's only the models that are poor.

The future doesn't scare me. My youthfulness marks time, but I discover in myself a zest for living that I didn't suspect. Will I see Philippe again? Yes, certainly! I will then have the strength not to hide behind easy quarrels. Our blows have now worn out. It took me time to learn that I could stand by myself! And now I would willingly kill anyone who would dare to pretend the opposite. Life evolves quickly and in spite of ourselves . . . Even the obsession about mediocrity does not seem to me like the mark of a superior intelligence. On the contrary, Philippe, I remember your fits of anguish, your feverish anticipation of the critics' words, fearing always the dreaded descriptions: vulgarity, mediocrity. Other people are sometimes like those merciless mirrors at dawn—they reflect an image that we dislike. I understand now that in running toward others you were running away from yourself. You chose people who were overly afflicted with your own peculiarities. You then believed yourself spared. Today I could tell you that I understand everything, and without my admiration for you being at all diminished. But you wouldn't tolerate it.

The center of my bed is slightly warm at last. I am in the middle of a nest. I try to identify with the rain. I am like it, yet I am not; and I pierce the marsh with a multitude of small, ephemeral, concentric craters. Like the rain I carry fertility. That happy thought goes with me into sleep.

Uneasy, I wake up as Bernard dashes into Hérouville's courtyard. I want to retreat; I think he is coming to get me because he woke up with an irresistible need to make love and is going to grab me by the hand and take me away by force. No, he must be coming to say good-by. The beginning of the term is near and he is leaving for Laigle. No, he knows that I am expecting a child and is coming to claim it back . . . Downstairs he stands rooted. Like a dumb thing, with a sheepish look, he holds down his head.

"You are coming. . . . to get me?"

"Yes, your grandmother. . . ."

"It has happened?"

"This morning, at five o'clock."

Mamie has departed at her special hour, the one at which she used to wake up so often from a too-short night. The hour she was accustomed to.

"Did she call your mother?"

"No, when Mother went to take up her breakfast, she was still warm."

She died alone, thinking of me who was not there. I had been caught out by time. The first autumn wind must have frozen the house. Mamie got cold. She was not able to wait until All Saints' Day. It is my turn to bow my head. Julie crosses herself endlessly and mumbles—I don't know what.

"Take me there."

"You must get some clothes. You'll have to stay there at least four days."

I gather my belongings with wooden hands. I think only of one thing. Mamie, my sweet, why did I have to find you if it were only for such a short time?

Immediately, I am angry with myself for such thoughts. Love is a miracle, one must not try to measure it. . . .

I suffer as if you had been a Mamie straight out of my happy childhood—a Mamie that I would have known and loved for so long that my memory would not have been able to fix the point of the departure of our delight. I feel myself violently shaken by a jolt of the country lane that Bernard has taken as a short cut. Why a short cut? What does time matter now! Periodically I tell myself that I'm having a bad dream from which I'm going to awake with a coated tongue and a heavy heart. I often had such a dream!

"I am going to postpone my trip to Laigle; you must go and

check all your windows at the house, Céline; two of them are rotten and won't hold out until the equinox. I spoke yesterday to the warden of the Goury lighthouse. He said that summer has gone and that we are going to have some heavy storms even after All Saints' Day. I also climbed up on the roof, there are some tiles. . . ."

I have to restrain myself from asking him if he is mad. But he speaks with the slowness that I have become accustomed to from Michel. Mamie is not yet cold—but death is in the scheme of things. Very soon, indeed, the autumn storms will smash their battering rams against the windows of Vauville. The dunes will be grazed by gusts of wind, and the seagulls will leave the rocks to find shelter in the villages. He has told me in simple words that I have a house and that I must take care of it because it is my own. I don't feel like snubbing him; as a matter of fact, I look at him now with a kind of gratitude. I let myself go and cry freely.

"I have shocked you, forgive me! Life continues, Céline. The death of an elderly person is quite normal."

"I know. Take care of the house and talk to the carpenter. We will talk about all of this after . . . the funeral."

"And my parents? What will you decide regarding them?"

He asks the question with dignity, but his voice vibrates with worry. After the roof, the parents! I would love to be able to concentrate on my grief.

"We shall see about that later on. You will take me to Cherbourg to order flowers."

"But they bury old people *without* flowers."

"So as not to cut the family inheritance by that amount?"

"No, it's the custom."

"Oh well—. I'll go against the custom once again!"

I am torn. Between Mamie and me there already lies a desert of lugubrious accessories: a priest, an attorney, a wooden coffin, the "last respects" . . . she is gone. I resist this truth and I'm anxious to touch her to convince myself that she belongs to me still.

Bernard's mother welcomes me with an appropriate face, but I don't greet her. I want to see. A stretched out body, the color of lead. A body left there, like a rumpled cloth. They have pulled down to eye level a nightcap whose strings enclose the depressions of her jaw. The lace of the cap barely hides a crepe bandage wrapped hastily under the chin to hold the jaw and prevent the mouth from opening wide. But the mouth, without her teeth, has caved in like a hen's nest. Mamie, you look like an old doll, poorly dressed in borrowed clothes. As for me, I am thwarted in my affection.

At this moment, I want to believe in the existence of the spirit. Yet the gracious spirit of my grandmother has flown away, leaving us a worn out shell. Then, I start crying in this room of death, like a bloody fool, as Philippe would say. With sobs which wrack my throat.

I don't know how long I have gone on like this. When Bernard's mother taps me on the shoulder and says that it's time to get Mamie ready. Everything in me revolts in disgust. *I cannot!* I tell her that I loved my grandmother too much and that I am unable to touch her. She will have to give Mamie the last bath without my help.

I go down to the garden. It's still raining. But the rain relaxes me.

I take a few steps. With the tips of my fingers I break off

the dead stem of a spent camellia. The earth has a long memory. Those who are born close to the soil are never able to deny themselves; inevitably they are betrayed by the first bush they come across, by a rain carried by a wind. Why did I half kill myself in a life that was not mine, having nothing to share with other wrecks like me but a complete lack of any future?

I am only that: a small peasant girl with round cheeks, holding on to her property, sad because autumn rains are like that, too, vivacious enough to resist her own attempts at destruction. There's no need to play the part of a Gioconda—but there is a need to carry out successfully one's own convalescence.

I look at the house tenderly. I will resist my first impulse to make out of it a museum dedicated to you, Mamie. The event kills the event. One day, this room where you now rest (that I consider a sanctuary), I shall use for a passing guest. Bernard comes to join me.

"Before the next St. Catherine's Day, I must root out all those camellias in the front yard."

"And what will you put in their place?"

"Some mimosas in the open air against the house and some geraniums elsewhere. When the carpenter comes, tell him to check the main door."

I speak in a firm voice. I cannot stop myself from looking at the house, for it now occupies a place in my life, out of all proportion to its real value. I have a roof over my head. You see, Philippe, you are no longer indispensable to me. You will be my guest, one day, maybe . . ."

I half-listen to Bernard, who says that he will come often to

Vauville, on all holidays, on Sundays too. Well, it hasn't taken long for me to become a good catch.

"You won't come. I don't want people to start gossiping. And I don't need you."

My voice is as sharp as a guillotine.

I leave him standing there. He has just decided the fate of his parents. I want to be mistress in my own house. And I don't want my son to know that his grandmother looks like a haystack.

Everything around me hurts me. The priest tells me that Mamie was "a good Christian," and I myself remember how terribly she hated intolerance. The attorney smiles at me and I know that he smiles at my new wealth, secure in lands, depreciated in title, devalued in paper worth. Yet like all old people, Mamie had a taste for shiny gold napoleons. He gives me an account of these "goldies"—he has the greatest respect for the yellow metal.

I am no longer there. I retire within myself, as I've done so many times before, to escape the reprimands of the convent sisters or Philippe's indifference later on. The nuns said that I was cunning—Philippe accused me of egoism.

Mamie is dead. My only concern is my grief, the emptiness that she leaves in me; I almost resent her for her defection. She is my first experience with the dead. For the first time, I am confronted with a body emptied of its life, awaiting corruption. So many struggles to get to that final nothingness! How petty our quarrels seem now, Philippe!

Michel arrives at last. He has never seemed as handsome as today in this house that smells of ashes.

"You are sad, Célinette?"

"Yes, very, especially to see Mamie shrunken so small."

"It's even more unjust for a person to be killed in the prime of life; for your grandmother, it's in the order of things."

He bows down before Mamie and then leads me out into the garden. We cross a field. We jump a low wall. The sea is in front of us.

"Why did you take me away? We'll shock the people who come to offer condolences."

Michel stops and grabs me suddenly. The rain streams down his forehead. He doesn't pay any attention to it.

"With your grandmother dead, will I be enough to keep you here?"

I stiffen under his grip.

"Are you still angry with me for being unable to love you when you were a child? You won't drag that regret along behind you all your life, will you? Your childhood has ended, Céline!"

No, childhood is never finished. I carry it. I hide it. I elude it. It encrusts itself. It is there—in my nightmares, in my horror of injustice, in my fear of humiliation. *My childhood.* The day when I'll be able to pronounce those words without tears in my eyes, I shall indeed be adult at last.

"The bank granted me my loan. I am going to restore those drafty barracks known as Hérouville . . . You failed in Paris. Stay here with me."

He speaks in a low voice, with spirit, but I feel that he has carefully weighed his words. I am afraid. I don't dare to answer. I know to what extent one can become the prisoner of someone and I don't want to be a prisoner any more. . . .

He chooses to ignore my silence and comes back to his idea with stubborness.

"I always wished to live near a woman who would love nature—early sunrise over the close, sundown on the marsh, the contact with the animals. We belong to the same race. This winter, I'll teach you to shoot, and we'll go hunting together."

"How do you think of me, Daddy? As a young woman or as your daughter?"

"As my daughter-boy. You often look like a boy, Célinette."

His plan allows him to think of an ambiguous answer. "I don't know exactly what you represent, but I don't want to give you to anybody."

"I belong to myself, Daddy."

"And then you belong to me, too."

I am not in a combative mood. I open Michel's oilskin and press myself against him. I link my hand behind his back. I bury my nose in the stitches of his sweater. I am warm. I feel like a little girl. I cannot help loving that haven that is open to me at last. Why should we try to determine the nature of the yarns our feelings when they are made up of so many contradictory threads? The main thing is love—never mind its aim or its way of expressing itself. Yet I am not a dupe. I don't want to ignore the fact that Michel is afflicted by an egoism as towering as a cathedral, by a passionate taste for liberty, by a sensuality that never allows scruples to get in its way. . . .

"And Marie, Daddy—how does she fit into your plan?"

He frowns, annoyed.

"You know her?"

"Yes, I met her while taking a walk with Grégole, we exchanged a few words."

"What do you think of her?"

"I think that you like her cooking and that you are bored in her bed."

He shakes me with his laughter. I pull out one of my hands from its shelter and trace with one finger his enormous jugular vein, swollen now by his laughter. The rain drizzles. Michel's eyelashes retain some tiny droplets of rain. As long as I can remember, I have never seen my father the prisoner of a collar or tie. He always wears a heavy sailor's pullover.

"You have a healthy way of thinking, my girl, I am fond of Marie, but she is no more than an ingrained habit."

What is it better to be: an ingrained habit or a fading memory? I ask myself, Marie, if such a sacrifice was worth the trouble?

"But still, she has been waiting for you for years . . ."

"If I understand you correctly you file me away; did you also book a room for me at the old folks' home?"

Abruptly he pushes me away and starts walking, his hands thrust deep in his raincoat. I have no choice but to run and catch him. I put my arm around his waist.

"Michel, don't sulk, you are much too big for that and. . . ."

I don't finish my sentence because he has lifted me up and I find myself lying on the sand.

"Calm down, stupid, look up."

I don't reason any more. I have always been more sensitive than intellectual. The sky atomizes tiny drops of rain on my face, and the water slides down ridges of my nose, settling in the corners of my eyes. I open my mouth and drink the rain, my head resting on Michel's shoulder. I see a gray sky, a sea

of mixed grays . . . my mood is gray, too, because near here
Mamie rests, in body only, and already I scold myself for not
having remembered that thick faille dress that she wore with
so much style. . . .

"You see, Célinette, our way of living is going to be close
to nature. You will go to Paris when you feel like being civi-
lized. Your doctor painted a very grim picture of your health,
but now you can drink if you want to."

I barely hear him trying to coax me. I remember Marie, her
face petrified with anguish.

"I'm afraid that Marie expects more from you than you
intend to give to her!"

"But my God, what do *you* care! I would feel happier with
you than with her. So, I choose you. I'm not the sacrificing
type. I'll continue to give her as much as I have in the past.
If it's not enough for her, she will take someone else! You'll see.
In life one must choose between oneself and others.

"And you choose yourself, of course!"

"I have never loved a woman enough to choose her first. You
certainly are the first one I have tried to be truthful with, and
you—you are my daughter."

Michel gets up and shakes himself like a hunting dog.
"Let's walk."

"No, Michel. I must go and receive Mamie's mourners."
My voice brooks no argument and he follows me.

"I like it very much when you call me Michel."

"And me, I abhor calling you Daddy."

"So, it's a deal, kid, we agree."

I look at him walking. I like the way he moves his body.
Everything is natural and spontaneous with him. His actions

have never been constrained by good manners. He lives freely. I must once more learn to allow myself to do the same. And it is possible, if I learn to accept my trials and tribulations. Why should I fight them, aggravate them, bother others with them? They are of my own creation. Philippe has been only the instrument. You have not given me solitude, Philippe, even though I have accused you of doing so for so long. I will tell you. Solitude is not something you acquire, you're born with it, like freckles. It is a natural aptitude never to be in contact with others. Life very quickly provides a pretext for developing that aptitude into an accomplished art.

We arrive at the house. Marie is waiting for us. We are dripping wet. The remnants of my hair are sticking to my forehead. She looks at us in amazement. She is dressed in black. The wind has blotched her complexion. She is dumpy and, under her dowdy hat, she looks like a member of a church sewing circle. It occurs to me that my mother could have looked like that. I have no regrets.

"Where are you both coming from, for heaven's sake? Céline! You are not in black?"

"Mamie would not have liked me in black! And your funeral pretenses disgust me. They give me the feeling that I'm transforming my grandmother into an Egyptian mummy. Don't forget, madame, you are only a cousin paying the customary visit—and not yet an intruding stepmother."

I have stopped her in her tracks. Michel is fascinated. Maliciousness when well expressed often impresses simple people.

I dry my hair before I reluctantly enter Mamie's room. Two candles are burning near the bed, their meager light elongating the shadows on the walls. This room, which used to be for us alone a universe of secrets and voices mixed together, now smells of holy water and death. I suffocate. I go down into the garden to cut some of the blue hydrangeas that are still in bloom. I strew them on the bed around her body; those flowers are a rampart of life.

Looking old, Marie has left with hunched shoulders. Michel did not accompany her to the gate.

The attorney arrives with his wife. She must be about my age. This young woman resembles a dead girl that I was fond of, a dead girl still alive: Emma Bovary. She is beautiful, but everything in her shows irritation at the banality of her life; she frowns, and her gestures to her husband show impatience, a fair pink face tells of her expectation. Michel inspects her voraciously. His eyes shine as he hastily details her slim, round body. That only too obvious desire makes my Emma blush. She looks like the February soil: dead for those who do not know that under her slim pellicle, chapped by the cold, life bubbles, impatient to spurt out. I feel ill at ease. Their eyes leave each other no more.

I do them the favor of taking over her husband. He has the face of a cuckold. It would be a shame to go against Mother Nature, when she predestined him for such a fate. Under the pretext of talking to him about the will, I draw him aside. Michel shows no sign of gratitude; he is too engrossed in what he's looking at. My interlocutor apologizes, he won't be able to attend my grandmother's funeral, but his wife will represent him. . . . Either Michel and his beauty will arrive late or he will dispense with the condolence completely. . . . I can no longer listen to this individual who now explains to me the choice of an investment. I grind my teeth. If I bit my lips, the blood would spurt. My poor fellow, if you are more scoffed at than I have been, I'll buy you yellow plums on All Saints' Day. One doesn't die of it. If one didn't forget one's sense of humor in panic, it would be funny. I have walked through fire. I am like those cider pitchers that are passed through the kiln to give them a porous glaze. I am able to laugh at everything. And especially at myself.

The attorney gets up at last. We go to retrieve his wife. She smiles, almost happy at what she regards as the promise of joy.

"Well, Michel Lemonnier: sold on the hoof, how much would she be valued at, that thing."

"What a pretty heifer!"

"You are going . . . to follow up?"

"Naturally! But Célinette if we live together at Hérouville I wouldn't like you to know about my conquests."

"There's no question about it, none of them will ever come through the gate of Hérouville, even if you father quintuplets. Furthermore, I demand from you a no-man's-land of at least fifty kilometers around the house."

"It's decided then, you'll stay?"

"We'll see. . . ."

"It's Marie?"

"Oh, go away. You take up too much room and you make too much noise. Just come back for the funeral."

He leaves. Mamie's house is emptied of life, of strength, of joy. It is no more than an open tomb. As night falls, the storm rises. The waves will soon break and crash on the Goury lighthouse, and in the night its luminous face will follow the flight of the foam as it changes into white flakes. I press my face against the cold windowpane, and water trickles down my cheek. I am not afraid, but I need life. Bernard comes hesitantly to say good night.

"Light me a fire in the fireplace Bernard, I'm cold."

"The wind is blowing from the sea . . ."

"Try, please; do it for me."

We pile up logs. His mother looks at me as if this were a mad sacrilege. I seem to remember that the custom in case of death is to extinguish the fire. I tell her to go to bed. We crisscross the branches of an old apple tree. Bernard begins to like the challenge. The gusts of wind drive the smoke down into our eyes. We cry, but we go on with our enterprise. And suddenly there is a miracle. A small blue flame dances, the sparks explode, the logs crackle. A feeling of well-being surges through me. I close my eyes. Mamie is there, she is not dead, I will continue to look for her like a she-cat whose little ones have been drowned. One day, the tenderness she gave me will germinate in me, will bring forth fruit.

Bernard settles me in the easy chair. He prepares me a cup of mint tea, helping me in spite of the rebuff that I have inflicted upon him. Why is it so difficult for me to loosen my lips to say thank you, even though deep within myself I am touched?"

"Sometimes . . . you are a monster, Céline . . ."

He stated that sad evidence in a tranquil voice, almost apologizing in advance.

"Not at all, but I am like the god Janus: I have two faces, one smiling, the other frowning, it all depends . . . being a monster is knowingly destroying someone who loves you."

I have the sudden feeling of treading on marshy ground. I

am not sure of my good faith, and my voice sounds false. If I pushed my deductions, I would have to confess to myself that I only play with this boy. One is always somebody's monster. I have the cowardice to look quickly for another subject of conversation.

"What do people here think of my father?"

"He is the best cattle trader."

"I'm not talking about that."

"He is a strong woman fancier. He nearly always chooses them young, well-known, and beautiful. He is a landowner and local councilman, so scandals are hushed up—'to the extent that you are powerful or insignificant' . . ."

I repudiate my political past to put a label on Bernard: the damned spirit of public school teaching. . . .

Michel is the man to conquer and defy, it's true; those peasants guess at it and envy it because they are incapable of the same audacity. The peace which follows those amorous victories must bore him very quickly.

The flames crackle. I am fascinated, as a wildcat would be. I love the heat. It comforts me to face everything including myself. The fire is healing.

Bernard will not go away. He will spend the night in an armchair by me. From time to time he gets up, half asleep, to revive the fire.

I throw my head back. Between my half-closed eyes dances a thin line of flickering light. Am I a monster? Am I going to tear myself away from my torpor with such a discovery? Why do so many people dread the confrontation with themselves. For fear of meeting a monster . . . or nothingness?

My sleepy eyes go from the orange flame to the big fair body that lies curled up beside me. I will try not to make him suffer. But to what extent is anyone master of the suffering she inflicts upon others? I will see him only on my "smiling Janus" days. Never again will I tolerate life with another person. The fire burns my cheeks, and my back is cold. Everything is duality and opposition. Philippe, if you were here tonight, without the presence of this fire and this adolescent, I would feel as naked and lonely as death itself. I would be able to tell you those exceptional words that sometimes erupt from the soul when circumstances either destroy our fear of what people may think or transcend it. I don't hate you any more. Nobody forces anybody to suffer. My suffering—I wanted it and accepted it with the thoughtlessness of youth, that makes us believe we have endless years, with the morbid taste for a suffering that we hope will introduce us to that adult world hitherto closed to us.

No, I don't hate you any more. It takes years to tie the tenuous and secret threads of a crisis. And then in a few hours, in a few weeks, the Gordian knot that choked us, gives way. Why? How? Maybe it is like the tides or childbirth—a question of the moon? The most amazing thing is what follows: a long silence, a total disengagement: the crisis now being over, we are left completely unprotected.

The fire lends a copper color to Bernard's golden hair. He will marry a teacher branded "an intellectual of the left" because she will vote Communist as a tradition and will make fewer spelling mistakes than I.

In a few days I will write to Philippe. I will notify him of Mamie's death. Philippe, I would like to make that familiar gesture that used to make you smile; I would turn your hand

and kiss the hollow of your wrist. I would, in such a way, thank you for that year of happiness that you gave me. It spun itself out like a dream of spring. Happiness feeds itself on innocence and wonder. It wears itself out with daily routine. I will have only feelings of well-being, knowing in advance the instability, the price, the end. . . .

This night is a long one. It seems to me that morning will never come. The paling fire weakens, and as soon as it does, a cloak of humidity slides over us.

My health will be my fortress. If I didn't have within me the life force that makes me face the wind and take the rain laughing, I would fear . . . hopelessness.

Bernard gets up to throw a log on the live coals. The light of the fireplace outlines his long body in a shadow. He is nice; it's funny—that precious quality to which Proust attached so high a price, when applying it to a peasant. I'm sure that he was virgin when we made love the first time. I could teach him Philippe's gesture. That's what is probably called "carrying on a tradition . . ."

"You don't sleep, Céline?"

"No, I am listening to the wind and looking at the fire."

"The wind is blowing up to gale force, or thereabouts."

"Do you think that the warden of the lighthouse is bored?"

"He's too stupid for that."

A sharp pain stabs my back. For a short time the cramp makes me gasp for breath. Bernard helps me to get up and I turn my back to the flames. What does such a night, the night I am supposed to keep watch over a much-loved corpse, resemble? The wind, with each gust, lifts up my roof, then sets it down again, abandoning it like a useless wreck. I am expecting a child, a Lilliputian conqueror who behaves like Atilla and makes me scream with pain, and if it were not for the light shadow of a dead woman in a closed room, Bernard would never be able to contain himself and would squash me under him until I gave in. . . . I believe in irony.

"It doesn't hurt any more?"

"No, I am going to try to sleep. Give me your hand."

I prop up my back against the cushions. We put our heads close together. We must look like two children ready to fall asleep. The flames throw spots of light on the ceiling. I recall that some lambs, latecomers, are stillborn on the day of the fall equinox; they are delicate and must be taken into the sheepfold for the winter. In a few days I'll go and buy a little lamb. When my son is born, he will be big, and when he takes his first steps, he will have his first lamb; my son will have the most beautiful of toys. Imagine that child: fair, plump, unsteady on his parted legs and clinging to the white fleece. I move my lips toward Bernard's hair, but he is asleep; in turn I fall asleep too.

When his mother finds us in the morning she bridles indignantly. There is no need to waste my time explaining that her son gave me infinite comfort merely by his presence. It would be easier to blow up the Goury light house with dynamite. Stupidity paralyzes and disgusts me. In a sharp voice I order some coffee and fried eggs and I invite Bernard to join me. The attitude of his mother changes immediately. She feels honored to serve her son at my table.

The carpenter brings Mamie's coffin. With his left hand he takes off his beret, white with sawdust. For the last time I gaze on the thin body of my grandmother. I place a bouquet of red roses on her breast. In contrast with their petals, Mamie's skin looks shriveled. The carpenter waits beside me. He has some long screws hanging out of the corner of his mouth and a screwdriver in his right hand. He is an honest and quiet man —ageless, slow, and without much future. He has so often coffined dead people!

I keep changing the placement of my bouquet. I don't dare to kiss the cold fingers. Instead, I kiss my flowers and I slide them between the clasped hands. I back up at last. The man looks at me out of the corner of his eyes. I do not move. He adjusts the cover of the coffin very carefully; pulling a red pencil from behind his ear, he marks with a little cross the closing points, slowly extracting the screws one by one from the corner of his mouth, he drives them in and tightens them. I notice that his missing index finger was severed at the base. His work finished, he salutes me and goes out, shaking with a strong hand each of the windows of Vauville, to determine those that will require his attention.

The following night, in accordance with custom, Bernard's mother watches over the dead body, telling her beads and sitting at the foot of the coffin, a coffeepot within her reach.

I go to bed with an "Ah!" of relief like a tired animal, a comparison that does not offend me.

The mass for the dead is held at the sailor's chapel in Vauville. It is soon full; all the village is there, though not from affection. But I am pleased that they honor my grandmother. Michel arrives at the chapel in good time. He is very dignified.

He watches for the effect that his impeccable behavior will have on people. I am impressed. The congregation is made up of simple people. The women are dressed in black. Once married, every Norman woman keeps in her wardrobe a mourning outfit. We are all, in a way, relatives by blood or prayers, so one might as well keep a mourning outfit just in case. We bury Mamie in the Cherbourg cemetery beside her daughter and her husband. The rain has stopped. The sky offers us a patch of pure blue, such as is found nowhere else. A blue so transparent that one drowns just by looking at it.

The ground of the cemetery slopes down sharply, and the gusts of wind from the previous night have swept all the flower pots down the slope against the wall. There is an accumulation of broken pots and smashed flowers.

The attorney's wife has come.

The sky is overcast again. People that I can barely see shake my hand . . . Marie kisses me . . . the attorney's wife smiles at me. The rain starts to fall, and people hurry away. I hear the car doors slamming. My father and I find ourselves alone, with Julie standing aside by herself. I had not noticed her. We are under some kind of porch roof surrounded by countless funeral accessories.

"Come on, Céline, it's over, we are going back to Hérouville."

I understand at last. Mamie no longer waits for me at Vauville. She is dead.

One morning, crossing a field, I pluck the first meadowsaffron, the earliest autumn crocus. Here we are—fall has come with her cool, early mornings and her misty evenings. Suddenly my green and gray country puts on crazy colors. The moor is covered with heather of a deep wine color, the poplars look like lighted torches, the woods redden, and at a distance one sees in the fields the piles of scarlet and yellow apples waiting for the bite of the frosts; soon they will be sent to the cider press. I cannot resist the desire to dig my teeth into them; their flesh is white and juicy, but they leave a bitter taste in my mouth.

I did not go back to Vauville. Bernard and the carpenter took care of the shutters, then Bernard came to say good-by. I accompanied him as far as Laigle in the car. In leaving him, I had the melancholic feeling one gets at the end of a vacation. Vauville is closed.

The gynecologist at Cherbourg has confirmed "my condition." After which, I climb the hill to the cemetery. Kneeling on the wet cement by the grave, I explain to Mamie that I must have a boy because if it were what Normans call "a pisser," I would take her to the swamp some dark night and leave her. I touch this little gravel garden with the flat of my hands. Mamie is lying there, I don't believe it yet. Philippe has sent me some very sweet condolences.

And the days pass. The way they pass in the country: slowly, regularly, marked by the same incidents happening time and again at the same hours. Prince had diarrhea and the vet came. We are the same age, and we attended kindergarten together. He pretends he remembers me. I hope he's lying! He makes several visits. He finally takes the time to sit down, settling into an armchair facing me. Looking at his contented attitude, I surmise that he was dying to sit there . . . I look at this frame of bones and muscles; the high receding forehead; on the temples the dark brown hair beginning to show patches of gray; the gray eyes starting to show life only after having evaluated his interlocutor; then all at once Francois' face opens like a window looking out over the sea, the fleshly lips loosen and uncover his teeth, planted in such an irregular way that they give that strong man the adolescent look of a growing youth. He is dressed like Michel—like all single men—in comfortable clothes that, by habit, are slipped on every morning. The elbows of his pullover are loose, and his trousers show the shape of his knees. I catch myself smoothing my hair to try to put it in order. I have a sudden desire to attract. And why have I the feeling that I've always known him? Yet I don't recall my early childhood. Did it really exist?

"So you were at the veterinary school at Maisons-Alfrot? I was at the Sorbonne."

"Yes. Then I came back to Caen for my military service and I settled in Valognes."

He bends his head. He thinks. No, he hesitates.

"I married the daughter of a Caen magistrate. She had sworn to me that she adored country life. I found my peasants once again with pleasure; I respect them, Céline. They are simple and straightforward. I like to chat with them, it is difficult to take care of an animal without taking a drink with its proprietor. Quickly, I developed a large clientele. They call me more often than they do the sorcerer! I had to install a telephone in my car. My wife became melancholic, she was bored. Then she started reproaching me for being a boor, for smelling of Calvados and cow shit. One evening, coming home, I couldn't find her . . ."

"And as for me, I came back to my father because my

husband smelled of other women! You see where the incompatibility of smells has brought us!"

I have made him smile.

We walk slowly toward the gate of Hérouville. He leaves regretfully I think. And, as for me, I would have liked him to have stayed longer.

I have bought a barbecue. Michel has installed it in a vacant stable. We often sit down on a bale of hay and lean forward, devouring quantities of crisp cutlets. Julie brings us some fresh cider and shrugs her shoulders as she watches these gypsy-like feasts. Today, I grill a chicken.

"Don't eat too much. Célinette. When I look at you walking, from behind you have the arse of a dowager."

"No Michel; I have the heavy walk of a pregnant woman."

"What?"

I no longer recognize my father's face. It is a mask of violence. My God, I hope I never showed such a face when I hated Philippe! The outlines are shriveled, the jaws are tense, the complexion livid.

With a voice that I want to be firm, I try to explain to him.

"Daddy, I am your daughter. I am expecting a child. He will be your grandson and the inheritor of Hérouville. For the first time, I know my place in society. I have always lived in the shadow of someone else. Yours . . . Philippe's that resembled yours. . . . I became a student in desperation, a Communist out of revolt, an alcoholic in imitation, a writer by identification and felt depressed the day I understood that those crutches were just a lure. I begin at last to be myself—a woman demolished, then rebuilt, piece by piece. The child: I want him! He will need me. And me—I already need *him!*"

"How did you do—'that'?"

Like my mother. She, in a hedgerow, I, in a sand dune. But I chose my partner, he didn't rape me. I made love to him, on my own initiative. I just forgot that children were made that way! Also, I was accustomed to a husband who did my thinking for me.

He gets up, pale with rage, wearing the crazy look of a male whose pride is wounded. I hear a car door slammed violently.

Julie bursts out of her kitchen, a saucepan in her hand.

"You offended him; he is angry. It doesn't matter, he is going to *her*. She always manages to ride the storm; but one day it will be like a hail-shower on March lettuce; he will tear her apart. And it will be God's justice."

"Leave the Lord where he is. Don't mix him up with your rancor. It brings bad luck to wish death upon others."

"Bad luck! I had my share of it. God is just, he doesn't give more than is needed."

I would like to believe Julie, in her assertion about divine justice, but God comes more easily if one prepares the way for him!

I give a leg of chicken to Grégole. The taste is new to her, and she is suspicious. She has been mounted by Letellier's dog, but Julie speedily brought the love making to an end with heavy blows from her dust mop. Do not be worried, my dog; this time they won't throw your puppies in the pond. The veterinarian will even come to deliver them, just to please me. We go for a walk.

We proceed slowly, both carrying our reprehensible pregnancies.

Michel's face haunts me. I read in his eyes the desire to slap me in the face. What must he say to Marie? Why does she put up with his fits of rage? To have the satisfaction of calming him down? But that is a false victory, people always dislike those who know their weaknesses.

Philippe will write to me very soon. We were to meet after All Saints' Day. Will he send me his book? How slow life is sometimes!

Anguish overcomes me. Everything seemed easy as long as the date of our meeting was still far in the future. Philippe's anger should be more violent than Michel's. I must not go to Paris. Our meeting must take place in camera. If we have witnesses, they will force us to play roles. Later, freed from those incidents that make up the present, I will perhaps judge my fears with a shrug of the shoulders. Yes, I will take the initiative in deciding this meeting: I am going to call Philippe! I will arrange a rendezvous at Caen; so he will be able to get there easily and we'll have a quiet conversation.

My two men—you have suddenly become my two judges! I am a strange one to be accused. I have no sense of guilt. My new heaviness weighs upon a soil I love. I have the sensation of being settled inside a skin that sleep, milk, and drizzle have made pink and smooth. Michel is stifled by Marie. Philippe will be stifled by his English woman. I retrace my steps. Hérouville is far away. Grégole is surprised by my sprightly step.

"You already? You must have walked really quickly. Your father has not come back yet."

"He'll come back tomorrow. It doesn't matter."

"You, at least, are at ease in your life. Other people's torments don't seem to bother you very much."

"And you, you worry too much about them."

"But I have nothing of my own!"

I look at her, astounded. It's true. Julie has nothing but her torment.

"So try to be kind Julie—you are not bad deep down."

"Kindness? No one ever showed it to me! It is a sickness of the rich. When I was eleven, they took me out of the orphanage and put me on a farm. I would have preferred to work in a shop, but it is said that 'peasants are too honest!' Your Aunt Amelie certainly wouldn't have been able to teach me kindness, God rest her soul. But she would have shaved an egg and worked a Pole to death."

Julie goes. The very sight of some individuals makes you shiver. She is one of those. She is devoted to me, but she speaks only bitter words to me, and on the days when her past without a childhood chokes her, she sneaks out of my sight like a blind bat. Michel has been the only joy in her life of nothing and that unique and consuming joy became monstrous. I will need enough courage to place her somewhere other than Hérouville. I want my child to be unaware of unhappiness. I want to build him a world of love so that he won't, like me, have warped judgment from the beginning, a judgement always directed at the worst option and then brought back slowly and carefully toward a favorable solution. I would have the joy of creating a happy human being. Oh, yes. I wanted to call Philippe! But where could I get in touch with him? Our own apartment is no more than a deserted vessel. So I call his editor and leave a message. They ask me who is calling.

I do not dare to say his wife. It's not true any more! I say "Madame Lemonnier." That slight deviation erases five years of my life—five years spent among monkeys, without sex, without appetite, without rest because their intellectual orgasms never permitted ten hours of deep sleep. I amused them in their idleness. Now, the very memory makes me desire to spit with contempt.

A car comes into the yard; it is Francois' Land Rover. He carries something in his arms—a small white ball?

"Well, look what I have for you. His mother is dead, so take her place. It is a new-born lamb, be careful when giving him a bottle. He will draw back on it as if he were drawing on his mother's teats. Push the nipple in well."

I hold the bottle tilted. By instinct the lamb draws back. Francois blocks the animal's movement. The milk starts to go down in the bottle. And a tiny white tail whips the air with satisfaction.

Both of us burst out laughing.

"You would be a good helper if you weren't going back to Paris."

"The day I go back to Paris, Prince will pee cider!"

The bottle is finished. When my lamb bleats, it would break your heart.

"He reminds me of a priest bleating from his pulpit."

"Ah! A bad Christian! Well, I shall call him Fenelon, it will be original."

My veterinarian has gone to sink his boots into the soiled straw of the stables. He is fond of animals. Between him and them there is a kind of complicity—his shelter is there, in that world in which speaking is unnecessary. Mine is in my books where dialogues are mute. Each of us, then, has his own way of tolling his knell.

"We see quite often nearby the veterinarian with the fancy speech of one who goes to confession. 'Fair women attract the male.' "

"Get out of here, old owl! There will be nobody to look after Vauville, if you continue. . . ."

The ring of the telephone cuts me short. Philippe, you have really surprised me this time.

"Céline, you tried to reach me?"

"Yes, we had a date on All Saints' Day; it's not far off now. The apples have been picked and the chrysanthemums are blooming."

"You are so lucky to be able to see the rhythmn of the seasons there, not just dates on the calendar! You're intending to come back to Paris, maybe?"

"Oh no! Absolutely not. I am settling down at Hérouville."

That piece of news reassures him, and I want to sound reassuring.

"Can you come up to Caen for a chat between trains?"

My proposal surprises him. I surmise.

"Are you in a hurry?"

No. I give birth in five months, but how can I tell him! It is delicate to announce to your husband that, legally speaking, we are going to have a baby. They should put me in a bag and drop me on the bottom of the Bosphorus, burn me at the stake, or stone me. . . . I have no inclination toward martyrdom. And all this is so unimportant! Philippe, you belong to a past that is losing its color.

"I have nothing to ask you but . . . I am expecting a baby."

"What? Are you crazy?"

"No."

"You had the audacity to do that to me? To *me?* Is that the best you could—"

"You couldn't be more wrong! I made myself a baby—I didn't think of you for a single moment! It's a happy incident and not a despicable desire for revenge or a sordid calculation. I would like us to part in a friendly way. After that, you'll never hear any more from me. Keep calm, Philippe. Take the noon train to Caen, I'll wait for you in the snack bar at the station.

"O.K. Let's settle this disagreement as soon as possible."

"May I ask you to be at least . . . discreet?"

"I will be extremely discreet."

He has hung up.

I'm not upset. I am not even affected. I'm only exasperated to have to give an accounting to a stranger.

Philippe, you a stranger? You have stepped out of my life. I imagine you more than I can see you, and you have no influence on me at present. Have I forgotten you? You, my closed world, the source and the end of my life? I have so often solicited and scrutinized your memory. In doing so I have used it up?

The months have passed over a worn-out wound of which but little remains. Forgetfullness. I am going to see you again . . . and it is as if I were to pass a garden I sold many years ago. Lifting myself up on tiptoe, I could catch sight above the wall of a tree that I'd planted, from which a strange woman would pick the fruit. I am now as peaceful as a cemetery. At the time of our last meeting, I had mistaken my tranquility for a sign of recovered health. I had forgotten what Proust says: "Every human being is destroyed when we stop seeing him." How could we escape this common law, when we are unable to escape time?

Is it because of Philippe's obliteration that Michel now seems to me to be indispensable? I don't want Marie to install herself between us, neither to judge us nor even to reconcile us; I must not give her the opportunity to exercise her influence for too long. And I fear the consequences of a hasty decision. I need my father.

Marie comes out on her doorstep. She looks me up and down. I am expected . . . and dreaded. I am sorry, but from the joust that we'll have, one of us will leave her bones in the dust. The stakes are too high. I will not lose.

"I've come to get Michel."

"You mean your father, no doubt?"

"Yes. My father's name is Michel."

"One seldom hears a daughter call her father by his first name."

"One seldom encounters old mistresses who have imagination."

Marie's eyes blaze. From that moment on no holds are barred.

"You've put on weight."

"Yes, but even pregnant, I am thinner than you are."

"You admit. . . ."

"And you—where did *you* go to acknowledge Michel's high jinks? I would merely have to go to confession while you would win the first prize of the Lepine competition.* But enough of this. I have come to get my father; he's been with you since yesterday. He must be out on his feet by now and dying of boredom."

"You are *common!*"

"No, I am realistic, ruthless, and sometimes truculent; not everyone has such qualities."

"Michel's place is here. We are going to get married."

"And you'll make him live in the three fields you rent? Michel needs Hérouville, and if he marries you, he will never again set his foot in it."

Marie blinks. A moment of truth is established for both of us. Both are accessories. Michel loves Marie as all men love their "back street" girls—by habit, by remorse, by low-down tricks. They are satisfied to be the holocaust of an entirely wasted life, devoted to their own pleasure, and perhaps also, because in the long run, she takes the place of their conscience. Looking at that woman they have sometimes spared from gossip with a lie, they have the feeling they have performed their duty.

Is Michel fond of me? I believe so. But also I represent Hérouville and Vauville where soon, from the top of the calvary, he will be able to count a flock of sheep without a shepherd, carrying his brand. He needs space to move in. I'll buy it.

At last he decides to show himself. You are not playing your best role, my father.

I pity you more for the symbol that you represent in my eyes than for yourself.

*An award given by the French Government for those who have very large families.

"Prince has the colic, Daddy, can you come?"

Marie's lips part to cry out, "she's lying," but no sound pierces the silence that weighs on us and rivets us to the floor.

"I'm coming."

I don't look at Marie. I climb into the car and start it up very fast. Michel knows that Prince has nothing. He doesn't show any sign of worry when he sees me take a direction opposite to the one leading to Hérouville. I drive him up to La Pernelle. The moor is purple with blooming briar, and the fog rolls in as evening blurs the horizon. One can barely make out the sea, flat as a steel blade, beyond the deserted lead-colored beaches. Like a mole who burrows down into its tunnel and becomes torpid, with eyes half closed, nature gets ready to sleep; she has delivered her fruit, improved the medlar with her first frost. Perhaps forgetfulness is like that—a repetition of the exhaustion that is death? We don't have enough lucidity to know that a Spring will follow. But the very rough winters mark the trunks of the trees with long scars, and it will take several springs to erase them.

"Let's go home, you are going to catch cold, and it's bad in your condition."

Those are Michel's first words. His voice is tender and protective. He has accepted the situation . . . and he is coming back to me. I do not answer; I am close to tears. A short while ago I would have asked you questions that would have cut you like a horse whip and would have set you up in opposition to me: "Why did you come back, for my sake or Hérouville's? Why do you accept this baby, for himself or because he will one day take over Hérouville?"

The world is empty, so empty . . . why empty it even more

with my intransigence? I do not sink in the affection that is called indulgence. No, I try to conciliate. Michel is fond of me. And he is also fond of Hérouville.

" 'My condition' is not a disease, Michel. On the contrary, you must force me to take long walks. I won't jump the hedges any more."

"Where will you have the baby?"

"At Cherbourg. I will not go back to Paris. I'll go to see my husband in Caen tomorrow at noon, to tell him. . . ."

"You'll come back the same evening?"

"Yes."

"I would like you to get through Carentan before the fog from the Bay of Veys settles down on the marsh."

Yes, there will be fog over the marsh, so I'll come back early. Those simple words have decided my future. I will meet Philippe one last time. I will not go back to Paris any more.

"I will call Matelot tomorrow morning. I want him to put in an oil burner; at least we'll have hot water and heat on the main floor before Christmas. January is often cold here."

"Yes, try to hurry him up a little. Tomorrow I'll put an advertisement in *Ouest France*. I'd like to find a couple; she would take care of the house, and he would help your bailiff to take care of the bulls. We could do over the annex; they would have their own quarters and we would have ours. I will send Julie to Vauville and I'll arrange a pension for her."

"You're right."

Every word, every silence is important; we are conscious of it. The fog has settled down, drowning all the shapes around us, darkening the shadows. It envelops us but we still continue to walk. A stranger could wander for hours without finding his way between the tufts of heather, turned gray. Our footsteps come out of the ground with a sucking noise. By instinct and at the same time, we both turn left. The road is there.

"I will not marry Marie. Or later, maybe, when we get older. We can still continue to live as we have done up to now."

I have the assured step of those for whom the future is simple. I raise my head resolutely and ask myself if at that moment I don't look like my boarding school friends who manage their farms like someone steering a boat. My past slowly disappears like the haze on the marsh, which gets thinner, disolves itself, and gets lost without people being able to say that it had been there.

"I will tell Julie of your decision tomorrow when you are in Caen."

"If you wish. But, I would be able to do it more tactfully than you."

"Yes, but I must do it."

We smile at each other, we are at peace. Michel's smile makes him look younger instantly. His features and his half-open lips have the carefree quality of youth. Why did life spare my father in such a manner? Like an old courtesan, life must have weaknesses. My mother's death must have been just another of those annoying incidents, quickly swept away by a flood of enjoyable loves that were never worn out by habit; I brought myself up without his even noticing my existence, and I can imagine him every morning of his life, eagerly slapping the rumps of his cows: "Let's go, my beauty . . ." My beauty, stepping aside heavily, flattered by his notice. And Michel getting high on the smell of leather, milk, and early morning mixed together.

146

It is night when we return in the car. The logs burn in the fireplace. How did Julie know that Michel was coming back? Perhaps through Léon's evening rounds?

As I am accustomed to do, I get up with the coming day. We have breakfast in the kitchen, but Julie's presence makes us tense. I am not distressed so much as irritated. Perhaps those years of serfdom give to the peasants a taste for freedom that, with us, turns into an excessive individualism. Perhaps the social consequences of my acts don't concern me. This morning, society resembles an iron collar, but I drink my coffee, my throat tight.

To relax myself or to kill time, I prepare Fenelon's bottle. Michel looks at me laughing.

"This house looks like Noah's Ark. What do you want me to buy you?"

"A white angora rabbit with blue eyes."

"Oh, come on! You'll have to wait for the Caen fair." What an idea, calling a lamb Fenelon! How can I enter him in an agricultural show with such a name?

He says anything at all, but his eyes are watching me. Both of us will have a hard day. How will he convince Julie to leave for an early retirement at Vauville? I fear his rough methods of getting rid of whatever shackles his life!

"I am going."

"Already?"

"Yes, I am going first of all to Cherbourg to buy a pair of trousers which fit! I don't want Philippe to think for anything in the world that I neglect myself. I have done that too much in the past.

"Well, have a good day. Are you positive you're coming back tonight?"

"Positive."

"Then, if we're sure to be together tonight, everything will be easy from now on."

"No, Michel. Marie has fed herself on wild hopes, and apart from us, Julie has nothing except loneliness. Be gentle with her, please. Life spared you. You have never known a great grief— you cannot predict people's reactions."

He puts on the face of a big unhappy child. I think of all the women who have flattered and fulfilled him, afraid that he might leave them. And he left them. They have known the fire; he never has.

I leave. Sadness is repugnant to me, like a pile of rags. I carry life within me. Death does not exist. Waiting for a baby is to deny death; and perhaps it is for that reason that I didn't fully understand Mamie's death. Such an event could concern me only if it were sudden and accidental. And yet I still don't believe it.

The end of October offers us some golden days, the early morning is fair and the heaps of apples, wet with dew, sparkle in the sun. I need to see Cherbourg. I like this city even though I was not born there. It is my chosen place. It resembles me. Like me, it is a little provincial, almost ugly, exclusive; but our melancholies harmonize. When the storm blows from the open sea and the waves break over the quay of Caligny, I gladly allow myself to be drenched and I feel free.

The fishing nets that the trawlers have dragged in the lower depths are drying in the wind. My eyes settle down, and my thoughts get lost . . . for how long will I be able to stay in such contemplation? Time then becomes of no importance and weightless. Our true birthplace is not the city of hazard in which life is given to us. It is the place we freely elect where —for the first time—our boundaries no longer choke us.

When I arrive at Caen, it is noon. All the station's snack bars are sticky, noisy, and smoky. Humanity here is sad, on the lookout, bound to time, a slave more than anywhere else. I am in a hurry to leave. The train enters the station, its mass obstructing the glass windows of the snack bar, which become darker still.

"What shitty place this is!"

"That is precisely what I was thinking. Hello, Philippe."

"Hello."

I smile at him. His is the well-known face appearing suddenly from the anonymous crowd, a sight for sore eyes. I see him without emotion, with gratefulness, because he isolates me from this unpleasant environment.

"Do you want to go somewhere else?"

"No, I must leave in forty minutes."

His voice is nasty. He stumbles on a reality less easy to deny than an idea or a resolution. And I am the one who forces that reality upon him. Without preamble, I hear him say that I have ridiculed him in the worst possible manner. He will look like an imbecile or an impotent, and I could very easily have spared him all this.

"You are like the vanquished, trying at all costs to come out of the battle with honor; if they are refused that, they are capable of the lowest kind of malice."

"Of course not. You won your war and I have been vanquished, I do not defraud you of your laurels. Keep them, my friend; they are to your credit. I didn't know that love had its veterans, who have memories as glorious as the others!"

"Anybody can scoff. I just wonder if you are out of your mind or without conscience. Try to imagine the situation you put me in. What will those close to me think?"

"That we had some tender meetings last summer! What could be more natural after such a long parting? Make a point of telling them that the mayor and the attorney in this part of the country served as witnesses to our morality. Come on, Philippe. What do these "others" amount to? Only a more or less brief episode of our life."

"How can you want to live in society and then reject it whenever it suits you?"

"I do not reject anything. I just don't want to let myself be dictated to endlessly. Remember how many of your enthusiasms for others were cut short!"

Two bitter arcs frame his mouth. Maybe the English girl has faded away? I look at him more carefully. Would he be the vanquished of another war? He wears an old tweed suit, shapeless, from constant use. His face is marked. He looks older, rather old-fashioned, a loner who rejects society, hoping to be spared by it in return.

There are undecided victories. Defeat teaches us how to avoid the blows, but love is like liberty. It is not meant for the weak.

I would like to run away. Everything has been said. You are dead, Philippe. The baby clears up the jumble of hesitations that would have been my load for who knows how long? Like the ashes of a love letter, burned with reluctance, that one hesitates to blow away because it is the last tangible proof of the past.

This conversational stalemate reminds me that nothing is ever secure. Not even grief. If that man I had loved so much is no more than a puppet unable to function for fear of people's gossip, if a great love can end over a spotted tablecloth—what, then, was the true value of his love and what was that man worth? I am not sure any more of the value of my memories. I do not dare, above all, to judge the grounds for my tears.

"Philippe, our quarrel is useless; you know me very well. You know that at no time did I have the desire to harm you. Had I wished to, my affection for you was such I would never have been able to do so. The law protects me in spite of myself! Don't let us part like this, in this filthy setting. Nothing is ever too important—it's you who told me that. At this moment, we are overwhelmed by the consequences of my actions, but we are also making ourselves ridiculous."

"Yes, what can you do against the inevitable? To tell you the truth, I have been indifferent to you for a long time. I was hoping that you could be completely erased. But you thwart my hopes. Come, let's go and have lunch and I'll take the next train."

I get hold of myself. I could scream with relief. We have lunch beside the quay of Saint Pierre, where the river Orne and its canal carry along to the sea the same dirty gray waters. We chat like two old acquaintances who have been separated by life for a while, each have had sorrows. We are without both joy and sadness. Philippe's face has lost its hard, masklike appearance; he is simply tired.

We both show the beginning of a smile. I resist the desire

151

Ogdensburg Public Library
Ogdensburg, New York

to say: Philippe, you are dear to me. Is it true? Or should I say: I am indifferent to you. I have known how to hate, but I do not know how to dislike.

I walk him back to his train. We are going to part. We look at each other astonished. Our gestures are in slow motion and are prolonged. Each of us carries away a part of the life of the other. Even if forgetfulness fulfills its role of vulture, even if I no longer remember the color of your eyes, even if I forget the sad years, recalling only the bright ones, my memory will sometimes cling to that five-years period. And yours will, too, Philippe. . . .

He keeps silent. I know from experience the exact meaning of his silences. He is questioning himself.

"I made a mistake, Céline. You were an animal. I wanted to train you. You revolted and then you sank into melancholy. I should have tamed you."

"You would have got tired of your trained animal. . . . Perhaps we came close to something exceptional. I met you too soon."

He shrugs his shoulders fatalistically, but his eyes no longer scorch me with their animosity.

As is his custom, he kisses my hand, in the hollow of my palm, and I take his hand. I turn it and, lowering my eyes, I press my lips against his wrist. People keep in mind for a long time the memory of their gestures. These rites of the happy days have survived our shipwreck.

He goes. And I suddenly have the feeling that my youth has turned its back on me.

I feel so lonely that I could cry. I am solitude personified. However, I have lost nothing since I didn't want to win anything. I stand there frozen: no movement can animate my heavy body.

Slowly I follow the road on which I know every belfry and every bend: Bayeux, Mosles, Isigny. It is too late—the fog has descended at the day's end. I am trapped in a sudden hole of semidarkness, a trail of haze, an opacity and unreality, the false night of a deep twilight. I hug the road, slowing down when passing a pair of headlights that I fear as a blind man fears obstacles. I am not afraid, but I think of Michel's anguish. Michel, one day you will be a demanding and possessive old man. Will the baby save me from the remoteness of Hérouville? And what else is left to choose from? Paris? Its crowds that isolate me, its stones that choke me, a man who will take me as casually as he would order an "espresso" when he has enough time to spare? I drive out of the fog as suddenly as I drove in. I feel a need to stop, to touch trees, to hear the leaves crackling under my feet. Here my solitude is free. Free!

When I arrive at Hérouville, Michel is pacing back and forth in the yard.

"Ah, here you are at last, did you run into much fog?"

"Very little."

His voice trembles, he is tense.

"Come, let's go inside. I prepared a fire."

"Where is Julie?"

"She's in her room, sulking like mad. Ah, what a day!"

We sit beside the fireplace. This time it is he who rests

his head against my legs. He is nervous. For the first time, I notice a long wrinkle running across his forehead.

Little does he care about my whereabouts. I am back, that's the main thing. But he. . . .

He explodes. He gets it all off his chest. He was told some bitter truths, he. . . . My eyes settle down and my pupils are almost hypnotized by the flame. A log crackles with the heat, breaks in half; its tree of origin laments, and its distant forest complains. I like the poetry of the fire. I dream of a man who would know how to love me with kindness, with strength, who would be able to spend silent evenings contemplating a wood fire. Perhaps he would call me "my bird"—not *chabraque*, especially not that! Perhaps he would like to make love beside the fire? Perhaps only his presence would make my room comfortable, under the squalls of All Saints' Day? Instinctively I rediscover my childhood habits. I dress up my night with sweet fancies, closing my eyes. I almost make myself believe in them. I would even have a house to protect my dream: Vauville. But the man? Will he come before that inclination I have, expecting from others only evil and disappointment that consumes so much that I'll be incapable of caring?

"What do you think? Can you recall anyone who was treated as I was?"

I pat Michel's hair, he thinks that I listen to him and share his stupefaction. I don't. I try to avoid a dialogue, the very thought of which bores me.

Yes, Marie had cried, begged: years passed in waiting, a life without a future, approaching old age. Michel stood inflexible, protected behind his egoism that her tears only aggravated. Then she screamed the words she had held in for so long, the daily sordidness, the cowardice, the vileness, the vices that she had encouraged but that humiliated her. I know well that sort of supplication that ends in a spray of filth. I cried it and screamed it long before she did. And how many others before us? She will resign herself to it. She will recommence waiting, watching for every tiny glimmer of hope. She knows very well that one day Michel will be older and then he will fear solitude. He will prefer to share his solitude with another.

He finishes talking at last. We drink a Calvados slowly, warming the glass in our hands. One has to drink to the emotions that one inflicts on others in order to get over them.

"And Julie, Daddy?"

"Oh, I settled that quickly, I just wasn't in the mood. . . ."

Julie. Upon such an unimportant life one can inflict anything. She took refuge in her room, as a wounded night bird looks for a hole in a tree, and she will not leave it as long as her fear is not overcome. How could it matter to her, without roots, to live somewhere else? For here she had planted her bitter roots, like those wild dandelions whose roots are as bitter as gall, so poor that no child ever bothers to pluck them.

I go up to bed sadly. Deep in my bed, I try to resume my dream. But it is no longer a little girl's dream. It is the call of a young demanding body that does not accept solitude. I have inherited my father's sensuality. Bernard was no more than a distraction during my convalescence. The need to love lifts me with an impetuosity that surprises me. I am a pebble rolled by mounting waves. With difficulty I find unwished-for sleep.

I am awakened by running footsteps on the stairs. Michel flings open my door.

"Don't leave your room."

I do not understand. This wild face and eyes—I don't dare to move. A car stops in the yard. Two gendarmes step out. I know them well, they often come to see Michel and are the same age as he. I hear them climbing the stairs with heavy steps. I don't dare to undertsand. I especially don't want to understand.

After a time that seems like an eternity, I hear the footsteps coming down again. I listen, my back to my door.

"You understand, Lemonnier, she thought that you had fired her."

"But, good God, I was sending her to Vauville to look after my mother-in-law's house!"

"She worked for you for thirty years, you could have kept her a little bit longer, and then you could have sent her to the old people's home. . . ."

The old people's home called "Hope"—why give a name like that to such a macerating vat where the old people wait for death, sitting on miserable chairs that don't belong to them?

I realize that I'm trembling and my teeth are chattering. I am unable to pull myself together. The car leaves. Michel comes into my room.

"Céline. . . ."

"I understand, Daddy."

He throws himself across my bed. I look with consternation at that great prostrate body. At fifty it is a little bit late to learn to face sadness.

Everyone suffers in his own way, each suffering is original and not comparable to any other. Michel's suffering is a bit like his animals': he breathes noisily, agitating his body with violent jerks, then lies prostrate.

"She wanted to hurt me; she knew that her suicide would put the whole countryside on my back. The people around here won't even try to understand. She will be cast as the victim and I will be the murderer. I will have to haul around that particular ball and chain behind me for the rest of my days."

Michel is right. Julie has paid the price of her hatred, but she took her revenge. The Normans kill their servants with work, pay them with reluctance, and feed them on the produce of the farm, but when these servants have "served" for a long time, they feel for them a kind of respect and open the family circle to them; the domestic is still only a poor relation at the bottom of the table, but nevertheless, a relation for whom one is responsible. Around Michel, the whole countryside will silently retire like the waves at low tide. The peasants know how to turn their backs with only their eyes. Then, the commentaries whispered from mouth to ear will create a legend around that death. Time will not save us. That body that once lived will weigh heavily upon us and crushes us.

"How did she . . . ?"

"She hanged herself."

I should have known. Here, in these parts a man takes his rifle, and a woman hangs herself. As for me, who had so often rehearsed my death—lying in a warm bed, a tube of sleeping pills in one hand, a glass of gin in the other—I would have had a sweet death, a deep sleep tinged with euphoria. Julie didn't rehearse, she wouldn't have known how to. Did she merely groan when the rope broke her neck?

I choke. I press myself against Michel to reassure him, to reassure myself also. People will make us accomplices in that evil, while we are accomplices only in our desire to be quiet and happy. We have been left behind by our egoism.

"It's strange, now that she's dead, I don't think of her as the person you have known, but as she was thirty years ago. . . ."

I would rather see him cry than watch his face, suddenly turned gray, twitching nervously.

Yes, Julie had her revenge.

She has bequeathed him torment.

I pat his cheek with the tips of my fingers, I have experienced this kind of pain before he has. In this I possess the rights of seniority. I would like to tell him, "Pull yourself together; one forgets pain, and one also forgets happiness!"

But the words of consolation do not come. I think of Julie. I am tied to her by the black kinship of those who have hated. I have pulled out of myself the remnants of that hatred, and this morning I feel immense pity for her who did not have either sufficient strength or youth to do likewise.

"Must I hand in my resignation to the local council?"

"I don't know; maybe . . . you should discuss it with Marie."

I would have liked, such is my love for him, to have heard him say: "I hope she didn't suffer." But one shouldn't continue to carry one's childhood dreams into adulthood; they don't grow up with you, and consequently they soon resemble myths.

Michel gets up like a sleepwalker. His steps will take him, as usual, to Marie. Once more, she will listen to him, calm him, and tell him that he's right.

Early one hazy, drizzling morning, we carry Julie to her grave. I wanted her to rest here in the vault at Gonneville. I would have considered it a sacrilege to open Mamie's vault for her. Yet, on the other hand, I would have thought her worthy of something better than a pauper's grave. Michel agrees without understanding all these subtleties. Only our farmers accompanied us, and they didn't like Julie. She used to ignore them.

Coming back to Hérouville, Michel lights a big fire to warm me up. Then he goes. I don't know where . . . but he will come back.

I snuggle deep into an armchair, offering my damp shoes to the fire. The heat penetrates me, and I lace my fingers together across my stomach. A happy smile comes to my lips. My baby is curled inside me, and I curl around him, our two lives making one. To feel better, with my hands I press the slight swelling of my skin. That contact stirs in me such an enthusiasm that I feel myself capable of the highest hopes—even happiness.

A shower of sparks shoots, crackling, out of the fire. The house is silent. Grégole lies down at my feet and lets the flames warm her nipples, now heavy with milk. Her time is near. I must remember to get in touch with Francois.

My eyes closed, I think of Mamie, then I dream of Grand-mère Phellie, the Chouan. How many times did she, like me, dry her feet near the fire. Like her, I was the follower of a lost cause; like me, cheated and robbed, she forgot her bitterness by walking along those sunken footpaths, sheltered from the wind, that are called "the hunts." Like the sauvagine, I am faithful to my wild marsh; its wild water-fowl's sleeping waters are my bright waters; I was never born to live on any other shore.

I think also of a stranger who resembled me. I don't recognize myself in her; I don't even find her sympathetic. I cry now for no reason. Tears held back, swallowed, crushed, and finally spilled; colorless tears—a dull stream.

However, I have a certain weakness for the last little tear; it is a minute pearl that courses down from my left eye. Puckering my lips, I catch it on the tip of my tongue. Its taste is that of almost-ripened cider apples. It's my final tear of irony.

Ogdensburg Public Library
Ogdensburg, New York

Bressy, Nicole
Sauvagine
595   EB   1972

WITHDRAWAL

Ogdensburg Public Library
Ogdensburg, New York